I AM JACK

Also by Susanne Gervay

SuperJack
Always Jack
Being Jack

Butterflies

I AM JACK

Susanne Gervay

Kane Miller
A DIVISION OF EDC PUBLISHING

Kane Miller, A Division of EDC Publishing

Text copyright © Susanne Gervay 2000
Illustrations copyright © Cathy Wilcox 2000

First published in English in Sydney, Australia by HarperCollins
Publishers Australia Pty Limited in 2000. This North American
Edition is published by arrangement with HarperCollins Publishers
Australia Pty Limited.

For information contact:
Kane Miller, A Division of EDC Publishing
P.O. Box 470663
Tulsa, OK 74147-0663
www.kanemiller.com
www.edcpub.com
www.usbornebooksandmore.com

Library of Congress Control Number: 2012931763

Printed and bound in the United States of America
6 7 8 9 10

ISBN: 978-1-61067-128-6

*To Malcolm Babbage, an inspirational teacher
who has made a difference to
the lives of his students.*

Mum's talking to Nanna. She said she'd only be a minute. That is such a lie. A minute means an hour in Mum time.

Oh no, I'm right. Mum has put the kettle on. She's going to the cupboard. Two mugs, crackers, cheese and tomatoes. Poor Nanna. Mum is always on a diet. Nanna won't like those crackers and cheese. That doesn't mean Nanna is thin, or even sort of average. No, she is definitely round and walks with a wobble and she loves cookies. I love cookies too. Mum is average in height and weight, except she hates her thighs and the tops of her arms. She is very funny when she starts to do jumping jacks in the middle of making chicken soup. Mum's short blond hair fluffs up when she jumps. My sister, Samantha, loves it when Mum does that and she jumps with her. It wasn't so funny when Mum did it in the parking lot the other day. What if someone from school saw her? I told Mum that I wouldn't help her with the shopping if she goes nuts like that in the parking lot.

"Mum. I've got to talk to you."

"Yes, Jack."

I give her the stare. She knows it is private.

"Jack, Nanna and I are talking about something important. Can it wait?"

No. It can't. "Mum, I need to talk." I grit my teeth. Mum can see I'm stressed.

"All right, then." Mum and Nanna look at me.

This is PRIVATE, Mum. Nanna's grinning at me. It is VERY private. I give Mum the eye. Like she has to know. I want to speak to her alone. But what does she do? She just sits there with Nanna, waiting. Mum always says I can talk to her anytime about anything. It doesn't look like it, does it?

Nanna interrupts. "What is it, Jack?" She smiles with her brand-new teeth. Her last ones fell out at the dinner table. She was so embarrassed when we went teeth-hunting under the table. I found them, but two of the front ones had fallen out and the left front tooth cracked.

"It's nothing, Nanna." But it is not nothing. It is really hard to talk about this and it has taken me ages not to feel guilty about bringing it up. I sigh loudly, but Mum just eats crackers and Nanna's a bit deaf. They start talking again. I give up. Mum doesn't care about me and I'm in a rotten mood. I may as well bother my sister. Samantha's one year younger than me. That means she's ten and a good person to bother.

Samantha's bedroom door is open. She's doing her hair. She's always doing her hair. How stupid is that? How can someone do their hair for hours?

"Just go away, Jack. What are you laughing at? Go away." Samantha's ears have turned red. You can see her red ears really well because she's put her hair back in two bunches. She ignores me. I run my fingers through my prickly hair. Mum's boyfriend, Rob, cut my hair two weeks ago with his new hair clippers. It didn't take long and it looked great. He shaved it close to my head. Sort of bald really. Mum was so mad and that's really rare for Mum.

Rob always gets a number two cut, which is quite short. Mum doesn't mind it on him. Why is she worried about my haircut? Usually I've got straight, brown, ordinary hair. My hair is growing out a bit and when I put gel in it, it stands up. I really like that. Mum has been better about my hair and laughs every time she sees it now. She calls me Prickly. Samantha says it looks great and she'd know. I think Samantha is going to be a hairdresser when she grows up.

I'm going to check if Mum and Nanna have stopped talking. I stick my head through the doorway. Notice me, notice me, pleasssse ... "Yes, Jack, darling." Mum looks at the doorway.

Mum knows she is not allowed to call me darling. The last time Christopher heard her call me darling, he kept repeating it for ages. "Darling Jack, come and have a look at this." "Jack, darling, let us play ball." "Darlingest, let us go to the park." Eventually he stopped because I ignored him and he got bored with calling me darling. When I told Mum NOT to call me darling, she said she wouldn't, but she doesn't understand why and she breaks down and forgets.

"Mum, don't call me darling. You promised."

"But you are my darling."

"Mum, we've had this discussion before and just, please don't." I look at Nanna. "Is Nanna going home now?"

"Soon, Jack. Do you *want* Nanna to leave?" That's such a mean question. As if I would hurt

Nanna's feelings like that. Luckily Nanna didn't hear the question. I told you she's a bit deaf.

"No, Mum. I want Nanna to stay," but just NOT NOW. Oh no, Mum makes another cup of coffee.

They go back to their endless talking. It's about Rob. This could take hours.

"Rob changed the oil in my car on the weekend." I can do that too, Mum.

"Rob helped carry up the groceries." You know I do that, Mum.

Rob took Mum to the movies on Saturday night, and left us at home to look after Nanna.

Mum is thinking of letting Rob move in. He already lives with us four days a week. That's enough. I like Rob a lot, but it's always been Mum and us before and, of course, Nanna visiting. Mum talks so much about him. I think she is sort of lonely. Not lonely for kids or Nanna or friends, but lonely for a dad. I don't want Mum to be lonely.

Rob, Rob, Rob … BORING. I'm going back to see Samantha. "Knock, knock."

"Go away, Jack," Samantha says.

"Say, *Who's there*."

Samantha huffs. "Will you go away if I do?"

"Yes," I lie.

"Okay. Who's there?"

"Samantha."

"Samantha who?"

"Don't you know your own name? Ha. Ha. Ha."

"That was very unfunny, Jack. Very, very unfunny. And you think you're a comedian!" Samantha goes back to combing her hair.

Samantha is in for it now. I make great jokes. "Look at your hair. Ha. Ha."

"What's wrong with my hair?" Samantha lifts up her chin. "Jack, you're being irritating."

"Oh yeah. Who'd wear their hair in pigtails? Only a pig. Squeak. Oink."

Samantha flicks the ends of her pigtails up, making her light-brown hair bounce.

"Leave, Jack. LEAVE."

I slump onto Samantha's pale blue quilt and make a big lump up at one end and a big hole in the middle.

"Get off my bed, Jack." Samantha turns her back on me and concentrates on sprinkling gold sparkles in her hair.

I make myself really comfortable and lie back on the quilt looking around. Samantha's room is the most color-coordinated, tidy room I've ever seen. Everything is in pastel and creams and pale blue. Her schoolbooks are piled on one side of her desk and her writing paper is right in the middle. Perfectly-framed pictures of a dolphin, a seal and a photo of Puss, our cat, hang on the wall. I look at the photograph. Puss looks great in it. Her eyes stare at you and her coal-black fur shines. Mum bought me a second-hand camera last Christmas. Not the automatic kind that does everything for you – a professional one. I can adjust the lens, focus on the background or the foreground, make pictures dark and mysterious, or light and funny. I can take double exposures. I took the best photograph of Mum holding up the sun.

My room is not very tidy, but it has character, definitely character. There are my schoolbooks piled on my desk. On my windowsill there are two jars with various life forms in them. I'm combining a few organic things. One jar smells. Something's not working, but the other one is the best. I've grafted an onion shoot onto an old, wrinkled potato. Imagine how famous I'll be if I make a new vegetable. I already thought of a name. Jack's Po-onion. Samantha said the name sounded like poo. She's so stupid – but I have had second thoughts. There could be other people as stupid as Samantha, so maybe I will call my new vegetable, Jack's Ponto.

I've got all my detention cards framed on my wall. Twenty-two detentions this year. A record. There is a toolbox in one corner. That's the neat corner. Anyone who touches my tools is dead meat. I'm making a coffee table for Mum at the moment and have had a few problems with the height. One leg is shorter than the other three and it is a bit wobbly. I know Mum doesn't mind, but it would be awful if she and Nanna always have spilled coffee, and Nanna is a bit clumsy these days.

My joke collection, car manuals and photographs are on the top of my bookshelf.

Mum's voice makes me jump. "Kids, Nanna's going now."

Samantha puts away her ribbons and brushes, then runs to hug Nanna. I follow her. My job is to help Nanna down the stairs. Our unit is up three flights of stairs. Nanna finds it hard to walk these days. Last year she had a bad fall and broke her arm. Sometimes I get sad because I remember Nanna playing ball with us and pushing Samantha on the swings. She can't do that anymore.

At last, Mum to myself. "Mum, Mum." She is making dinner already and Samantha's helping her with the pasta sauce.

"Later, Jack, darling. When I'm finished making dinner."

"Don't call me darling, Mum." I slump onto the couch. Later. That's a joke. Rob will be here soon and then there will be dinner, washing dishes and I have to have a shower and there's homework and television. Mum will be tired. There'll be NO time and I HAVE to talk to Mum.

I think I'm in BIG trouble.

It's morning. I go back to bed. Moan. My head is a volcano of burping lava. Oh no, I feel a big burp coming. Groan. It has blown up in my head. Can't move. Ooohhhh.

"You haven't got a temperature, Jack." Mum puts her hand on my forehead. Her hand is hot. I look up at her. All I can see is her blond hair fluffed up like it has exploded. It always looks like that, except when she tries to smooth it down. Then it looks like a flat explosion with bits out the side.

"Do you think it's something you've eaten? You might have an allergy." Mum's hair is a fuzz ball.

Ooooohhh, I feel another burping lava attack. I hold on to my head and look up pathetically. "No," I whisper. It couldn't be breakfast. I didn't eat anything different, just the usual bacon, eggs, two sausages, fried onions, grilled tomatoes. I only had one piece of toast with honey. I had whole-wheat bread to be healthy. The two raisin muffins had nothing on them except margarine – oh yes, and a bit of cinnamon and sugar. I squeezed two oranges in Rob's special old-fashioned juice squisher, to wash it all down. He lets us use his juice squisher when he's not here. I did have a green apple afterwards. It was pretty sour. Maybe that gave me a headache. I look at Mum. She bought the green apples from Mr. Napoli's fruit and vegetable market next door to where we live.

Mr. Napoli's fruit and vegetable market used to be called a fruit shop, but he has spent a lot of money renovating it. Mr. and Mrs. Napoli and my friend, Anna, worked like hyperactive ants, painting and pulling out shelves. I helped with the shelves. Now you can walk around the aisles and pick your own fruit and vegetables. Plus there is bread, juice, nuts and eggs that are for sale. We always get the farm fresh eggs, even though they cost a bit more. That's because of this documentary we saw on battery hens. Thousands of hens were kept in huge barns with no daylight, crammed into cubicles, pecking each other. I'd really hate that. No place to get away from everyone. Nowhere to escape from other pecking beaks. Mum and Samantha closed their eyes, which is typical, but Rob watched the whole thing, like me. Actually, Rob put his arm around Mum. I don't know if I liked that.

Mr. and Mrs. Napoli's shop is now called the Super Delicioso Fruitologist Market and he is a fruitologist. When Anna told me that, I tried not to laugh. I couldn't help making a couple of jokes about it. Mum says I'm a comic. I do find things pretty funny sometimes and I'm always collecting jokes. I've found a few good ones on the Internet, but I mostly like to do original stuff.

This fruitologist joke is mine. "Is your dad a tomatologist? Or an orangologist? Or a pumpkinologist? Or an eggologist?" I have to admit that I went on a bit. Anna was getting pretty mad. Her curly black hair started bouncing up and down as she shook her head. From experience, that is a dangerous sign, but I couldn't stop. The jokes sort of had a life of their own. "Onionologist, carrotologist, melonologist ..."

"You're a complete idiot, Jack." Anna's big brown eyes sort of looked like cannonballs aimed at my head. "Those jokes aren't even smart." She turned up her nose at me. She's a bit like that. "I can't be bothered with you." I know I shouldn't have asked her this, but with her nose turned up and her yelling at me that I was an idiot, what could I do?

"Anna, your dad's not a fruitologist, geologist, proctologist. I know. I know. Peanuts, walnuts, coconuts." I was laughing so hard by then. "That's it. Nuts. Ha-ha. A nutologist. He's a nutologist." She got so angry that she stormed out of her parents' shop. She wouldn't talk to me for four days. That was pretty tough because Samantha and I go nearly every second day into Mr. and Mrs. Napoli's Super Delicioso Fruitologist Market. Anyway, I told her twenty times that I was really, truly sorry. I wore her down until she eventually said it was okay, except I am never allowed to mention *nuts* around her, which is pretty difficult when I have to buy pistachio nuts for Mum.

Anna is eleven, like me. We've known each other since we were five when Mum, my sister and I moved into our third-floor unit. Mum had to take on a huge mortgage, which meant she was always working to pay off the loan and Samantha and I were always sent to the Napolis' fruit shop to play with Anna. So, even though Anna's a girl, she's nearly my best friend. I hardly tell anyone that, except Samantha knows.

Ohhh, my head. Moan. It hurtsssssss. I feel exhausted and slide deeper under my covers into my bed. I like my bed. It's new. Well, sort of new. I got it when Rob bought Mum a king-size bed and Mum gave me her old double bed. Samantha has a single bed. Rob said I would need a double bed soon because I'm going to be nearly six feet tall one day. I'd like to be *over* six feet tall. It would mean that no one could push me around. I think of George Hamel. A shiver wriggles down my spine. Everyone knows you have to keep out of George Hamel's way unless you are in his gang. Who'd want to be in his gang – unless you're stupid or a loser?

Mum puts the blanket over me. "Just close your eyes, while I get some medicine." Mum always has something in her kitchen cupboards that will cure me and everyone else. It's a pretty wild kitchen. Everything is bright orange, except the countertops. Mum says the orange cupboards were the only thing Dad left us. Mum took them with us to the unit, but she bought the countertops. Mission Brown countertops – the color is supposed to represent earth (that's the brown bit) and soul (that's the Mission bit). To be honest the countertops look like mud. Mum says it was a very meaningful color when she was a hippie. I think Mum is still a hippie.

I've seen photographs of Dad and Mum when they were younger. They're funny. Dad wore small, round, metal-rimmed glasses like John Lennon and multi-colored shirts and shorts, and open leather sandals. Mum wore crazy-bright long dresses. She still wears crazy colors. It's a bit embarrassing sometimes. Mum talks about changing the kitchen colors, but has never gotten around to doing it. She hardly ever looks at those old photographs or talks about Dad. I'd like to ask her about him, but she goes quiet when I do and I can see that she wants to cry. Dad married someone else and we don't even know where he lives. I can't remember him much except he liked to use methylated spirits for cuts. It kills the germs and nearly killed me. It really stung.

Mum doesn't use methylated spirits. I don't know if it's because of Dad, or because she hates stinging (I do), or because she's got her own special cures. She uses tea-tree oil for itchy bites, talc for the rash I sometimes get from my belt rubbing against my bellybutton, sorbolene cream for sunburn, hot, salty water for red lumps anywhere on me, and ginger ale for headaches. I don't know how it helps, but Mum is back with the ginger ale. I half sit-up to drink it, then lie back again. Mum kisses my cheek, then strokes my head. It makes me feel better. "There'll be no school for you today."

No school. No school. I can feel the volcano simmering down, except for a stubborn throbbing in my eye.

Mum starts patting down her hair. That means she is upset. "Darling, I've got to go to work." Mum used to be a library assistant, but it was only part-time. Since we moved into our unit, she has always worked full time at the twenty-four-hour, seven-day-a-week supermarket attached to the service station. If I stick my head out of my bedroom window I can see the gas station and the Napolis' Super Delicioso Fruitologist Market. Our unit has two and a half bedrooms — one room for Mum, one room for me and half a room for Samantha.

Samantha's room used to be a dining room. Samantha doesn't need more space because she is short. She's not going to be really tall like me. Our unit is at the front of the building. I really like my bedroom. I can see everything that happens on the street — kids hanging around, people buying hot bread from the old bakery, car crashes, fire engines screaming down the road …

We know most of the shopkeepers. Mrs. Jonah always gives Samantha and me a caramel each when we buy milk, and Mr. Green always gives us the best bacon, and Joe always gives me the best deal when I rent movies. The other day he put in *The Lion King* for Samantha and an action-packed movie for me for nothing. Mum hates action films. Too violent, she says. Luckily Rob watched it with me.

"I've got to go to work. Will you be all right, darling?" I don't mind Mum calling me darling when I'm sick. I nod weakly. That molten lava is still moving around in my head. "Samantha can stay home with you today to keep you company."

Samantha's already arrived with the Monopoly. She sits at the end of my bed. There's plenty of room.

"I'll call Nanna to come over at lunchtime. You can ring me if there's a problem."

Excellent. Nanna is good at Monopoly and she'll bring over some cookies. I look sadly at Mum and hold my head.

"It could take another day before you're better."

I nod again weakly. Another day. My head

calms down a bit more with that news. No school tomorrow.

No school. I feel the erupting volcano stop.

Rob's here. Rob works in spare parts for cars. That is so great. We talk about mag wheels and power steering and V8 engines. When I'm old enough I am going to buy a dump of a car and do it up. Chrome bumper, super-charged engine, five-on-the-floor gears. Poor Mum rolls her eyes. Get it. Rolls. Rolls … ha-ha …

Do you know why the man rolled his car into a lake?

He was trying to dip his headlights.

Mum's not mechanical. She just doesn't GET IT, but she *does* get very mad when we say that to her. "Mum, you just don't GET IT." She really doesn't GET IT when Rob jokes. Some of his jokes are bad and, I have to say it, rude.

Rob and I look at each other because we know Mum doesn't really understand, especially the rude ones. My jokes are only a bit rude. This one is adapted from a joke Christopher told me. He isn't very good at jokes, so he gave it to me to make into a masterpiece.

Once upon a time, there was a little red man, who lived on a little red street, in a little red house. One morning this little red man woke up and looked out of his little red window at the little red sun. He thought it was a glorious little red morning. So he jumped out of his little red bed and skipped down his little red hallway into his little red bathroom. He threw off all his little red clothes and turned on his little red shower. While he was splashing around in his little red shower, he heard a bang on the door. He quickly turned off the little red shower, put on a little red towel, ran down his little red hallway, opened his little red front door and saw there was a little red newspaper stuck in his little red rose bush. He bent over to pull it out. As he bent down his little red towel fell off.

The lady sitting at the bus stop who had been watching the whole thing, jumped up and ran across to the other side of the road and was immediately hit by a passing truck.

The moral of the story is:

Don't cross the road while the little red man is flashing.

Rob likes that joke. Even Mum does.

Samantha runs out of my bedroom into Rob's arms. He swings her around and around making her laugh, BUT it's me who is sick. I need the attention. Samantha is always pushing in. I struggle out of my bedroom. Rob has just given Mum some pink carnations. He is hugging her, BUT it's me who is sick. "Rob, Rob, I've got to tell you how sick I've been. Did you bring the car manual I wanted? Rob, I've got to tell you a new joke I made up. Rob ..."

Samantha's carrying out a vase. It's her job to arrange the flowers. Mum is checking the rice. "It's sticky white rice tonight. You won't get an allergy from this, Jack," she says. "It will help your headache. Maybe you can go to school tomorrow."

Samantha butts in. "Jack was all right today, Mum."

I put my hand over my right eye and moan loudly.

"Well, we'll see how he feels tomorrow."

Rob shakes his head and jabs his knuckles into my arm.

"Ouch, that hurt."

"I think you've got your mother worked out all right. You don't look sick to me."

I knuckle him back.

Mum looks up from the rice cooking on the stove. Her hair is fluffing out. "Stop that. You're supposed to be sick, Jack." Mum flattens her hair. "No fighting inside. Actually, NO fighting at all." Mum always says that because of her hippie days. There's a great photograph of her in our album holding up a sign – *Make Love, Not War*.

Samantha grabs the cat because she knows wrestling is serious business. Last time Puss nearly got squashed when I fell on her.

Rob laughs. "This isn't fighting. We're messing around and Jack's feeling better." We wrestle in the family room and Rob gets me onto the floor. I'm too strong and pull away from his grip, but then he grabs me in an armlock. I break away and grab him now. Rob's laughing and pleading. "You're too good for me, Jack. Too good." I release his arm and he jumps me. "Never let your guard down, Jack."

Mum's shaking her head, making the bright-green clip in her hair wobble. It matches her bright-green shorts. "Dinner's ready."

The rice is definitely white and sticky. It sticks to the top of my mouth like glue. Samantha rolls the rice into little balls and makes a rice man with a carrot for his nose and peas for his eyes. Mum laughs and makes an even bigger rice man – Rob eats the head off and we all laugh.

Usually we have un-sticky brown rice. Mum's made her soy sauce and chicken special and there is passion fruit cordial and brown bread. It is Mum's usual excellent dinner. Rob likes Mum's cooking and tells her. That makes her smile. The pink carnations are in a glass vase right in the middle of the table, so it's hard to grab the bread without hitting them. Mum likes the carnations there.

After dinner Rob and I have to clear the table and do the dishes. That's a bad thing about Rob. Before Rob, Mum did them every night and I got to watch television, or go downstairs with Samantha and see what Anna was doing, or work on my plans for the car I'm going to build one day.

Rob is a maniac washer. It's like an operation. When Rob started coming over, he bought special implements for the dishwashing operation. A long-handled scrubbing brush, three new dishwashing sponges, a stainless steel pad, good quality detergent and a cleanser. The water has to be so hot that it nearly burns your hands off. Dishes are scraped, then rinsed, then piled into categories. The cutlery is in one pile, the big dinner dishes into another, the pots into another, the glasses … Then we're ready to go. The BIG WASH.

The dishes do look good after we have washed them and the sink is very clean afterwards. I guess I don't mind helping and it means Mum doesn't have to do it.

Even though Rob makes me do the dishes, there are some okay things about him. Rob messes around, wrestles, sometimes does a bit of rugby with me. Mum's not good at that sort of thing, but she does take a ball down to the back of the building and throws a few baskets with me. Mum got the board in the building to let her put up a basketball hoop. Anna and Samantha play basketball too sometimes.

Rob's taking me to see a big rugby game next week – without Samantha, luckily. We're going early to get a good place on the hill. I've never been before. When he asked me I felt funny. My friends, Christopher and Paul, go a lot with their dads. Their mums complain about it. I wanted Mum to complain, but she didn't. She was just so happy and said she'd drive us there and pick us up. Rob said "no thanks" because this was between Rob and me.

We have to do things there, like eat hot dogs with ketchup, talk about the game, stand up when a goal's kicked, shout and boo and cheer. We'll probably meet Christopher and Paul and their dads. We might hang around afterwards drinking lemonade (for me) and just one light beer for Rob. (He'll be driving.) There'll be rugby stuff to do.

Can you believe that Mum won't let me play rugby at school? I know I'd be good at it. But no. Mum says, "I don't want your nose or anything else broken and you've got headache problems as well." As if that matters. "Jack, you know if anything happened to you ..." Mum gets choked up and I have to hug her. She needs me. What can I do?

Rob tried to tell Mum. "Let Jack play rugby if he wants. He's already eleven."

"That's right. He's ONLY eleven. Don't interfere, Rob."

"Don't I have a right to say what I think?" They had an awful argument and Rob stormed out of the house. Mum cried and I felt rotten and Samantha said it was my fault. Later Rob came back, but it was horrible because they didn't speak to each other for the rest of the night.

Mum makes me play soccer. I like soccer, but it's just that I'm too slow dribbling the ball. I would be okay at rugby because I'm getting bigger and stronger. Five Saturdays ago, the rugby and soccer teams were playing. Mum came to watch me play soccer, of course. It started off badly and got worse as the day went on. Mum didn't wear her bright-green shorts. She wore something nearly as bad. A rainbow-colored cotton dress. She loves that dress, mainly because Rob told her she looked pretty in it. She does look pretty in it, but it's just that she doesn't look like the other mothers. Then she forgot her promise and called me "darling" in front of the whole rugby team.

After the game Mum spoke to the coach and gave him a long lecture about how good soccer is and how dangerous rugby is. I tried to stop her, but that's pretty impossible when Mum is on one of her causes. What was worse was that George Hamel was standing around and heard it all.

George Hamel is a rugby player. He's a front forward. A big front forward with muscles that stick out of his chest like hamburgers. He's a real meathead. Joke. Joke. Do you get it? Hamburger. Meat. Seriously, he's one big guy.

I avoid George Hamel ever since I beat him in the handball game. It was bad enough beating him, but I made this joke. It was a great joke, except George Hamel didn't like it much and that's dangerous. George Hamel isn't like Anna. He's not the type to forgive you, even if you beg.

I was pretty hyped up after beating him at handball. My team was cheering for me and I called out to George Hamel, right in front of his team: "Do you know how to improve your handball team?" I waited until everyone was listening. Then I put my huge foot right into my mouth. "You should leave it."

Everyone laughed. Luckily, the sports teacher was there because George Hamel would have made me one of his hamburgers. That was last year, but George Hamel never forgets.

When Mum left to go to the car while I took off my soccer cleats, George Hamel started in on me. "Do you always do what your mummy says, Jack? She looks so weird. You're a weirdo." He was laughing. His mates were laughing with him, adding other stupid comments. "Yeah, Jack does what his weird mummy says, don't you?" "Jack's scared of rugby, poor little thing." "Might get hurt, mightn't you, Jacky?"

I hated them calling Mum weird. I hated it, but George Hamel was snarling by then.

Actually, he looked like a hyena leading a pack of hyenas. He'd just lost his last game and was in a rotten mood. George Hamel is never allowed to lose anything. I could see he was going in for the kill. "Don't want my little precious Jacky to get hurt. Precious little Jacky. Precious little Jacky." That George Hamel's stupid. He can't even think of new insults and keeps repeating himself. He actually started drooling and the pack behind him were drooling.

"Does Mummy wipe your

butt too?" Unluckily for me, he seemed to really enjoy the word "butt" and kept saying it.

I started to get a headache. What could I do? There were at least six of them snarling. The coach was on the other side of the field. Mum says to ignore ignorant people like that and they'll go away. I tried to ignore them, but it is pretty hard when George Hamel's standing over me and he's got to be six feet tall. He didn't go away. I wanted to say something, but my voice choked up. I just walked off. Didn't say a word. I could hear George Hamel shouting out, "Go on, run away! Run away, Butt Head! Butt Head, Butt Head." Everyone could hear "Butt Head" all the way across the field and out the front gates.

Mum was waiting in the car, smiling at me. "I was really proud of you on the soccer field today."

Mum knows nothing.

George Hamel and his pack wait for me these days at the school gates. They sing out "Butt Head, Butt Head," laughing so much that some of those meatheads fall over themselves. Don't the teachers see them, hear them? Teachers are supposed to stop them. What am I supposed to do? Fight? Maybe I could take on George Hamel. I'd probably be killed.

I want to talk to Mum, but she's got no

time. Too busy. She's tired a lot. I've got to work this out myself. Mum depends on me. Well, there is Rob now, but I'm the one she counts on. What would she do if I didn't carry the shopping up the three flights of stairs every week? And what about all the light bulbs and washers I've changed. Without me we'd be living in the dark with a flood of water sloshing through the family room.

I hate worrying her. She's been doing two shifts at work for the last three weeks. Mum says she wants to pay off as much of the mortgage as she can and she'll have more time with us soon. When will that happen? Never. Never. Mum will just work and work and the mortgage will never be paid off and I'll be dead. George Hamel will kill me.

Ooooohhhh, my head hurts. Those lava burps inside really thump. I can feel my head bursting.

Mum is stroking my head. "Wake up, Jack. You're late for school. Come on, Jack, you have to get up. Samantha's already dressed."

I open my eyes slowly. Yes, yes. I'm late. My plan has worked. Last night Rob talked Mum into making me and Samantha go to school today, even if I was sick. But I'm late, late, late. George Hamel and his idiot mates will be in class by the time I get there. I'll be safe. At least, for a while.

Rob's already gone to work, so it's just Mum, Samantha and me. I knew Mum would let me sleep in. She always does after I've been sick. I hold my head and struggle into the shower. Mum is sympathetic. This is going to be the longest shower in history. Oh no, Samantha's thumping on the bathroom door like a maniac. What does she want?

"Hurry up, Jack. I need to go. Urgently. You HAVE to get out of the shower. I'm bursting."

"Jack you'd better finish that shower." Mum knows that Samantha has a weak bladder.

"Jack, Jack, I HAVE TO GO now, or I'll go in your room." Samantha's banging and banging at the door. She means business.

"Okay, okay, don't panic." I wrap a towel around myself and emerge from the bathroom clean and late, very late. Samantha nearly knocks me over in the rush. A giant moan of relief comes from the bathroom.

By the time I'm dressed and arrive at the kitchen, Mum's special breakfast for sick kids is ready. Oatmeal. Not the instant kind made in the microwave, but the big rolled oats kind, cooked in a pot on the stove. Delicious. There's brown sugar, milk and a dab of butter.

"This will be good for you, Jack."

I slide onto the kitchen stool next to Samantha who's already wolfing down her oatmeal and she isn't even sick. Her bowl is on the place mat I made for her birthday. I took an excellent photograph of Puss and had the photograph laminated on the place mat. I made up an excellent joke that's printed on the place mat. Samantha thought it was a very clever joke. Mum did too.

What do you get when you cross Puss with a kangaroo?

A purrfect jumper.

Rob gave me my place mat. It's the back end of a 1964 Valiant with a chrome bumper, wide red taillights and a license plate – 000 JACK. I guess it's a bit corny, but Rob had it specially made for me. I really like it.

"Hurry up and finish the oatmeal, Jack." Mum's washing the oatmeal pot at the sink. She doesn't do as good a job at washing as Rob, but then Mum is always in a rush. "I'll drop you both at school. I'll be late too if we don't get moving." Mum's hair is fluffing everywhere as she grabs her bag. I guess it's late enough now, so I move fast. My lunchbox, books and a tennis ball are stuffed into my bag and I grab my wallet. It's got the front door key, bus pass and emergency phone money to call Mum.

"Come on, Mum, Samantha." They're so slow. I jump two steps at a time down the stairs.

"Don't do that, Jack. You'll fall," I hear Mum calling out after me. She always calls that out. I jump four steps in one go at the bottom. I'm aiming for a record. I think I'll try for five steps next time. Samantha can jump three steps at a time.

Mum's car is a nine-year-old sedan that needs a new muffler. We sound like a farting elephant as Mum drives up to the school gates. I'm really, truly lucky that George Hamel is in class already.

"If you feel sick, Jack, call me."

"Sure, Mum," as if I would call. Mum could lose her job and then she'd never pay off the mortgage and then we'd be thrown out of our home and end up on the streets and then Rob would leave us because he couldn't afford to support us all. No, I'll never ring Mum even if my leg is half-hanging off or I have a giant nail in my foot or George Hamel smashes me to pieces. I shudder. George Hamel.

Mum scribbles a quick note to my teacher explaining why I was away from school. Then she scribbles a note for Samantha saying why she was absent and why she's late.

Samantha walks with me into the yard. It's not a good idea to walk into the yard with your sister, especially a younger one. You get harassed by idiot guys for that. Someone should tell them that half the world is made up of females and guess what? A lot of them are sisters. Anyway, there's no one to see us now AND I've got to face George Hamel soon. My head is aching. Samantha's chattering about Puss who she loves and Mr. and Mrs. Napoli who promised to give us a mango each this afternoon. Samantha adores mangoes, but Mum doesn't buy them often because they're expensive.

"See you at the bus stop, Samantha."

"I'm glad you're better, Jack," she says as she runs across the grass with her brown pigtails bobbing and her skirt flapping in the wind.

BIG BREATH. My head hurts. Oooohh. That lava is burping. There's sweat on the palms of my hands as I stand outside the classroom door. Mr. Angelou's voice booms right through it. "Open your math books." I can see Mr. Angelou through the glass pane in the door. He actually looks like an angel. A big, ugly angel. He's very tall, with a round stomach. His head is mostly bald with a few tufts of thinning black hair and he's got rosy cheeks. All he needs is a halo and a pair of wings, except he isn't an angel. He's tough. Mr. Angelou has been known to give kids a thousand lines to write – *I must behave.* He gives detentions, makes you run around the field fifty-five times, forces you to stand outside the staff room for the whole of lunch and the worst thing, calls up your parents. Mr. Angelou is tough.

"Sorry, sir, for being late." I hand Mr. Angelou Mum's note.

He reads it. "Right, then. Hope you feel better. You'd better catch up on your work."

Christopher and Paul nod at me. They sit at the same desk. As I walk past Anna's desk, she smiles. I'm not allowed to smile back because she's a girl. It's stupid. Normally I couldn't care less what everyone else thinks and I'd smile, but not today. George Hamel is sneering at me.

I just wink at Anna. We'll see each other at the Napolis' Super Delicioso Fruitologist Market after school today. Wish it was the end of school NOW.

Mr. Angelou's bald head shines like an egg under the neon light. He looks like he really has got a halo. I must be delirious. George Hamel sits right behind me. Mr. Angelou assigned our desks at the beginning of the year and there's no way anyone can move. Mr. Angelou turns his back on the class to write formulas on the white board. "Butt Head." "Butt Head." "Butt Head." "Butt Head." Whispers are coming from everywhere. I can see Anna. Her brown eyes are big and staring, which means she is worried. Me too. Christopher and Paul have their heads down working out the math problems. I think they don't want to see me.

Mr. Angelou turns around quickly. "Did anyone say anything?"

Dead silence. I'm going to be dead when the bell rings. I've got to have a strategy. Think, think, think. Right. I'll grab my apple and tennis ball, race up to Mr. Angelou to ask him to explain the work I missed and walk out of the classroom with him. George Hamel and his mates won't have time to catch me. Then I'll race outside to the back of the bathrooms and meet Christopher and Paul there to play handball against the far wall.

I look at my watch. Timing is everything. Okay, I've got my apple and ball. My head is throbbing. Noise from kids packing up. "Butt Head." "Butt Head." "See you outside. Ha. Ha." Race to Mr. Angelou. Sweaty palms. He looks surprised. Explains the work I missed as we walk together through the door. Run, run. I catch a glimpse of George Hamel and his mates from the corner of my eye. He's so dumb he won't realize I've got a strategy. Puffing. My chest is going to burst as I speed like a racing car down the stairs, past the staff room, over the field to the bathrooms. I look around. No one is following me. Made it. Made it.

Panting, I lean against the back wall. I look out from behind the wall. No George Hamel. Kids are playing in the yard. Girls are sitting in a circle on the grass. George Hamel won't bother them. I stuff my green apple into my pocket. Even the thought of it makes my head pump. That must be what is causing my headaches. No more apples for me.

As Christopher runs across the grass, he calls out, "Have you got the ball?"

I hold up the tennis ball. Then it's serious playing. I throw the ball against the wall and Christopher slams it back. Paul isn't very coordinated and misses, making Christopher scoff. "Too slow, too slow." The handball game always ends up with Christopher and me thrashing it out. Sometimes he wins. Sometimes I do.

The bell rings. Christopher walks with me towards the classroom, past the girls getting up out of their grass circle. "Are you all right?"

"Don't know, Christopher." Christopher doesn't offer to help me and I don't ask.

Through clever tactics like walking in a crowd, standing next to Mr. Angelou, racing out before anyone else has packed their stuff in their bags, I survive the day. But something strange is happening. It's not even George Hamel anymore. Kids who don't even know me are calling out, "Butt Head." "Butt Head." "Butt Head." It's like a game and I am the target.

I sit near the girls in the bus. Anna is two seats in front of me, next to her girlfriend.

Samantha is behind me next to no one because she's bringing home her artwork. It's a collage of branches, petals, aluminum foil, buttons, colored paper and shiny nuts and bolts. Rob brought home the nuts and bolts from work. "Do you think Mum will like it?" Samantha taps me on my shoulder.

Mum likes everything Samantha makes. I bet Mum puts it right in the middle of the table so that we can't see what we're eating tonight. I don't feel like teasing Samantha today. "Mum will think it's terrific, Samantha."

I help Samantha off the bus with her collage. Anna carries Samantha's bag and we move quickly away from the others. On the way home, we walk past the supermarket where Mum works. She always waits for us at the window. Once we stopped off at the park and went home another way. Mum waited and waited for us to walk by the window of the supermarket, but we didn't go that way. That afternoon Mum left work early and ran all the way home and up the stairs and banged against our door crying. She thought we had been stolen or in an accident or something horrible had happened to us. She couldn't stop crying for a long time and we cried too. Mum said we were the most important things in her life. We have never done that again. Even if we go to the park or to the Napolis' Super Delicioso Fruitologist Market we always wave at Mum's supermarket window first.

Samantha and I run up to Mum's supermarket window and wave. Mum blows a kiss to us before going back to work. Anna waits behind a tree, then runs quickly with Samantha's collage past the supermarket so Mum won't see it.

Mrs. Napoli is waiting for us with three big, yellow mangoes. They are so sweet. Samantha is disgusting and it drips on her clothes. Mrs. Napoli runs to get a wet cloth. Nothing drips on Anna because she's used to eating mangoes.

Afterwards, we throw a few baskets into the net at the back of my building. Anna really concentrates. She gets nine out of ten baskets. I only get six and Samantha gets seven and my head feels a bit better. Tomorrow is the weekend.

Saturday. Saturday. Hooray. I'll just check out my organic life forms. Hmmm, my Jack's Ponto looks good. There are green sprouts coming out of the top of the potato head and it smells like an onion. This is going to make me rich for sure.

I had better bang on Samantha's door. "Hey, Samantha, get up." Puss jumps off Samantha's bed and nearly knocks over Samantha's lamp. That cat is fast when she's heading for the kitchen and food. Food? I'm hungry. Nanna should be here any second with our breakfast. I love Saturday morning breakfasts. "Are you getting up, Samantha?"

There is this angry grunt from under Samantha's sheet. "Get lost."

I'd better tickle her. We've got to start moving. Samantha tries to kick me with both legs. Is that nice? Right, she's in for it now. Tickle. Tickle. "Get up or I won't stop."

Samantha is very ticklish and I know just how to torture her by going to the most sensitive spots. "Jack, stop. I'm up already. Stop it, Jack. Stop it."

"You got up just in time. That's Nanna's footsteps." Nanna shuffles along these days. Just as I exit Samantha's room to find Nanna, there's a huge slam of the bedroom door behind me. The door nearly smashes into me. It could have knocked me down and I could have crashed against the opposite wall with the handle jabbing into my spine and I could have been paralyzed. I'm lucky to have escaped. Samantha has a bad temper, if you ask me.

"Nanna, Nanna, what have you brought us?" I give Nanna a hug. Nanna misses hugs ever since Grandad died. That was seven years ago. He died of a heart attack. It was quick and Mum says that Grandad didn't suffer, but Nanna did. She didn't have time to say goodbye and tell him all the things she'd forgotten to tell him when he was alive, like how she thought he was strong and the best husband and dad, and how he told the best jokes and made everyone laugh.

When Nanna takes us out to the cemetery to see Grandad she talks to him. I do too because I can remember Grandad. I want to tell Grandad about George Hamel. A shiver goes down my spine. No. I don't want to think about George Hamel. Grandad had a moustache. I'd help him fix up his car with my hammer and wrench. They were only plastic, but that doesn't matter. I remember Grandad saying that I was a fixer and that it was a great thing to be a fixer.

Nanna's bought flaky croissants and a fresh baguette from our bakery for breakfast. Oh, Nanna's got three giant cookies as well. Nanna takes the apricot jam from the cupboard and margarine from the fridge. She has oranges for orange juice. She used to squeeze them for us, but these days her hands are sore with arthritis and I do it on Rob's juice squisher. "You're such a helpful boy, Jack. Just like your grandad."

Saturday mornings are always Nanna mornings. Mum works every Saturday in the supermarket. "Look what I have for you." Nanna is the best special buyer in the world. She buys watermelon for half-price and bought the jeans that I really wanted at the end-of-season sale. It helps Mum out and it means that I can eat watermelon in jeans that fit. But there is one tiny problem with Nanna's specials.

Socks and underpants. Everyone needs socks and underpants and I have to tell the truth, I lose a lot of socks. Just one of the pair usually, BUT I never lose my underpants.

Samantha grumps in. "Why did you wake me up, Jack? I'm tired now. It's your fault." Grump, grump. She gives Nanna a hug, then drags a chair over the tile so it makes this horrible screeching sound. Ugh. Nanna doesn't hear, of course, because she's rummaging in her bag and you already know that she is a bit deaf. It's sort of funny, but Nanna doesn't think she is deaf. She thinks people don't tell her things, but in some ways she is happier because she doesn't want to hear a lot of things. I wish I didn't hear things too. Butt Head. Butt Head. I put my hands over my ears. Nanna puts on the TV so loud that everyone in the building hears it. You can even hear it down the street. Nanna thinks there is something wrong with our TV because of the volume. It doesn't go loud enough for her, but she knows we can't afford a new TV, so she puts up with it. Nanna loves her TV shows, especially the soaps.

Smiling, Nanna takes out four pairs of socks for the price of two, and six pairs of underpants for the price of one. "They're very fashionable, you know." Fashionable? Mum would love them. They're purple. Bright fluorescent purple. Glow-in-the-dark matching socks and underpants. "I don't think they'll fit, Nanna." I hope they don't fit.

"I bought one for everyone with some extras."

Samantha nearly chokes on her orange juice and as she coughs, her pigtails start bobbing up and down.

"Are you all right, Samantha?" Nanna is always so kind.

Samantha nods.

"Look, look." I make a significant discovery. "There's one pair of underpants here in your size, Nanna."

Nanna's face lights up. "I didn't notice that."

"You can wear purple underpants too." Nanna likes that idea and shuffles into Samantha's bedroom to try them on.

She arrives back in the kitchen smiling. "Perfect." She lifts up the back of her dress to prove it. We're nearly blinded by the fluorescent glow, but yes, Nanna is wearing her purple underpants and they fit.

Samantha puts on a pair and so do I. "We're the family that lights up, Nanna."

Nanna thinks that's funny. Samantha giggles. Samantha's in a better mood because she is stuffing herself with a giant cookie. So is Nanna. I had better take my cookie before Nanna and Samantha have seconds.

"If we get robbed, we'll just have to flash our underpants and we'll blind the robber." I get into my joke mood.

"Ha-ha, ha-ha, ha …"

"Doctor, Doctor, why do I keep seeing purple in front of my eyes?

"Tell your Nanna to pull down her dress."

"Ha-ha, ha-ha, ha …"

"What's purple and slimy and goes hith?

"A snake with a lisp. Get it? Lith … lisp. Lisp." I lisp through my cookie and end up spitting a bit on the table. I can't help it because jokes and a mouthful of cookie are a pretty dangerous combination.

Samantha tries to say I'm disgusting, but she's laughing so much she ends up spluttering cookie onto Nanna's plate. Luckily Nanna can't see so well either and she doesn't care anyway.

It's a fun breakfast. Then we start on Nanna's Saturday morning routine. She mops the kitchen floor. Samantha has to get the mop and bucket from the laundry room. Nanna tidies the kitchen while Samantha clears the table. Nanna vacuums and I move the chairs so she can get the vacuum hose underneath them. She dusts the blinds. I do the high parts. Lastly, Nanna empties all the wastepaper baskets and puts the trash in a bag for me to take down to the garbage can. Exhausted, Nanna kisses us and says what great children we are and gives us five dollars each. She makes herself comfortable with a cup of tea in front of the TV. "Be back before your mother gets home," she always says.

We hug Nanna. Then Samantha and I race down the stairs. Samantha actually jumps three steps in one go at the bottom. I jump six steps. "Come on," I call out to Anna, who's waiting for us in front of the Napolis' Super Delicioso Fruitologist Market and we're off.

I'm in charge of adventuring. We're heading to the beach for serious rock climbing. Anna's carrying her usual backpack, which Mrs. Napoli has filled with drinks, fruit and nuts. It is really difficult asking Anna for a nut since it has become a banned word. I just have to point a lot. Anna's got almonds. My favorite.

I tell Anna about Nanna's purple underpants and we laugh all the way down to the seaside. The weather is just right for rock climbing. A sunny day with a cool breeze. Samantha's brought her bucket to collect interesting shells or a starfish if we find one. I've got my pocket knife combo attached to my belt. It's made out of stainless steel and has a knife, bottle opener, scissors, can opener, corkscrew and file all in one. Rob gave it to me last Christmas. That's when I knew he liked me a lot. He knows I need it for all the things I do and it cost a lot of money. He wouldn't have bought it for me if I was just nobody. I knew Mum was happy when he gave it to me because she put her arm through Rob's and rested her head against his shoulder. Rob did go overboard a bit when he bought Samantha a new desk and a swivel chair. That cost even more than my pocket knife. That doesn't mean he likes Samantha more than me.

"Come on." I lead the way across the rock platform towards the sea edge. "Just follow my footsteps. Be careful." There are a lot of pot-holes, boulders and sandstone outcrops. Samantha fell into a crevasse last time and scraped her knee and I had to carry her on my back all the way home.

Anna stops. "Jack, come back and look at this." Samantha is already next to her peering down into a rock pool.

Anna usually finds interesting things to investigate, so I hurry over. It's an enormous jellyfish. It looks like a big blob of gooey paste with tentacles hanging from it.

"Yuk. It's disgusting." Samantha shudders. "I don't want that in my bucket."

I get a stick and hit the water. The blob of jellyfish contracts, but its tentacles just float with the ripples of water. A small crab clambers between the cracks in the rock pool and a sea anemone. I bend down and dig into the water with the stick.

"I don't like the jellyfish. It can sting you." Samantha holds Anna's hand.

"I wouldn't let it sting you, Samantha." I stand up. "Let's look at the waves."

The water crashes over the edge of the rock platform spraying sea into our hair. It smells like salt and when I lick my lips I can taste the salt too. A fisherman throws in his line and waits to catch something. There should be bream around. I like the sea even though there are jellyfish.

Samantha takes her bucket to look for shells, but Anna stands with me looking out at the sea. I wish I didn't have to go to school again. I wish I could just stand here forever and never go back. Quietly Anna tugs at my shirt. When I look at her, she has her hand pressing against her lips.

"Is something wrong?"

"Yes." The wind tussles her hair and she pushes it back. "They're like jellyfish at school, aren't they?"

"What?"

"Jellyfish with stingers." She hesitates. "You've got to tell me. What's happening at school?"

"I don't know what you mean." But I do know. I'm in trouble.

"I hear them calling out names at you. It's horrible," she whispers. "And I'm supposed to be your friend, and I've said nothing, done nothing."

"You can't do anything. It's my problem. I'll fix it."

"I don't think you can."

"Sure I can." I feel a hot pain in my head.

"I want to help."

Anna can't help me. I know that, but somehow it makes me feel better that she wants to.

Samantha runs over to us. "Look what I've found." She shows us a strange orange-striped helmet shell that swirls into a peak with a creamy, smooth inside. We look around and find more shells. I use my pocket knife and carefully scrap off seaweed from a very interesting sea snail shell that Samantha wants.

Afterwards, we eat Mrs. Napoli's juicy peaches sitting on a rock looking out to sea.

◆ 6 Karate Kid

Sunday night. I'm lying in bed watching my Jack's Ponto growing. It's going to be a monster. I know I'll be rich. I had the best weekend. Rob took us all out for dinner, including Nanna. Mum liked that a lot.

I had a big plate of fries, lots of coleslaw and a huge T-bone steak. Mum never lets me get T-bone steak. Usually I have lamb chops or sausages because it is cheaper. I don't mind or anything, but it is great having T-bone steak. Samantha had a cottage cheese and pineapple salad because she copies everything Mum does, except she did have fries. Nanna had mashed potato, pumpkin and one sausage because of her teeth. She can't eat chewy things even though she has new teeth.

I'd hate to lose all my teeth, that's why I brush them twice a day and sometimes three times. Samantha doesn't. She's going to be sorry when we go to the dentist.

Rob took us to the movies after dinner, which turned out to be really unfair because of Samantha. We had to see what SHE wanted. Rob always does that just because Samantha holds his hand and makes cards for him saying, "You're the best dad." Well, Rob isn't our dad or even our stepdad yet. Mum's still talking about him moving in full time.

I sort of want Rob to move in, but I don't. I don't need a dad, except sometimes I get tired of changing light bulbs. I don't mean that really. It's not the light bulbs. It's just that it would be good having someone else, a grown-up helping Mum. Nanna does help, but she's old. I don't want her to be old. She needs me like Mum does. A dad would be something.

George Hamel joked about Mum and said who'd be stupid enough to marry her. He said that in class when Mr. Angelou couldn't hear and had his back turned writing on the white board. Lots of people would marry Mum. Lots and lots of people would. I didn't say that back to him. I should have. George Hamel said my real dad left because of me. That was the worst thing. I couldn't speak.

Anyway, I don't know why today was great. We didn't do much. I just worked on Mum's car with Rob. We did a grease and oil change in the garage. Mum brought us cold drinks and said we looked like grease monkeys and then handed us two bananas. Mum's funny. That's where I think I get my great sense of humor.

While we worked on the car, Samantha went off with Mum to the gym. Rob's been helping out with money and Mum says she can now afford to pay for classes. Samantha wore exactly the same black shorts as Mum, the same blue T-shirt, the same white socks and tennies, the same headband. I couldn't help laughing. I was going to say something clever, but Rob kicked my leg and said, "DON'T." I wonder how he knew. It was only going to be a tiny joke. It wasn't that bad.

You look like twin plums going to the gym.

There'll be a lot of plum pudding wobbling around.

That is pretty funny, isn't it? I think I'll use it the next time they go to exercise class.

For lunch, I helped Mum make tuna and tomato sandwiches and passion fruit cordial, and I carried out the picnic blanket to the backyard. Samantha found the basketball. Rob brought out a folding chair and read the newspaper. Anna came over and we threw basketballs into the net. Mum played. She's good at it because she used to play at school. Of course, Samantha's playing at school too. I told you she copies Mum.

Rob fell asleep in the folding chair and Mum fell asleep lying on the blanket beside him. This was the photo opportunity of the year. I ran upstairs to get my camera before they woke up. I took the greatest photographs of Rob snoring with his mouth open and Mum next to him with her blond hair fluffing in the wind and her purple socks rolled down to her ankles. You couldn't see her underpants, but I know they were purple too.

It's late. I hit my bed with a hammer blow. I've got to concentrate on tomorrow. The start of another rotten week at school. I pull out the magazine I bought with the five dollars Nanna gave me. *Karate: Self-Defense and You*. Mum will be really angry if she knows about this, but it is self-defense. I have to protect myself, Mum. I have to.

Karate is the martial art of unarmed self-defense in which directed blows of the hands and feet, striking with lethal kicks and punches, accompanied by special breathing and shouts, are dealt.

Speed, strength, technique, alertness, timing and use of surprise are essential to karate.

I have done a few practice kicks, but it's hard. I know I'll be able to do it if I study the drawings. Hand chops, knuckle punches, hammer blows, finger jabs, jumps, stamping kicks. I'm so tired. I'll just read a bit more, a bit more, a bit … zzzzzzzzzz.

Panic. The sun streams through my window. Samantha's singing in the shower. Mum is making breakfast. Rob has already gone to work. Monday morning. My karate magazine slides off the bed. I can't go to school. My head hurts, hurts, hurts.

Mum is not interested in my headache. "Non-negotiable," she says. "School's on."

It starts on the school bus. "Butt Head." "Butt Head." "Butt Head." It echoes along the aisle as boys walk past. There are a few thumps on the way. George Hamel isn't even on the bus. Anna isn't either. She's probably helping in the Napolis' Super Delicioso Fruitologist Market. Samantha's frightened and I force her to sit at the back. She doesn't want to. I make a mental note that I'll get up early tomorrow and walk to school. How do I get off the bus when it stops? I can't stand up now because I'll get sandwiched between the guys in the aisle. That's dangerous. Maybe I'll finger jab one of them in the kidneys. Ohhh, my head really hurts. The bus jerks to a stop. I make a dash for the door, shoving as hard as I can. Suddenly there's a big surge forward. I lose my balance. I stumble down the bus steps trying to grab onto the sides. I half-make it and land on my knees, ripping a hole in my trousers. It stings, but I'm out and I run.

There is no way I'm going through the school gates today. Then I see her. The librarian walking to the side gate. I race towards her and offer to carry her books. "That's nice of you, Jack." She chats about good books to read, while my heart's throbbing like an enormous blind pimple. The library is open every morning break, every lunchtime. "There's always someone here to help you find a book. A librarian and an assistant." I stand close to her as she unlocks the library door. It's like a revelation. Sunlight floods the big room with its shelves of books arranged alphabetically. Tables and chairs are neatly placed in the center of the room. There's an alcove with computers and another alcove with the copier and audiovisual equipment. Paper ducks flap from the ceiling and posters hang between shelves. A safe house. The throbbing subsides. I've found a place to hide. A safe place.

I stay in the library until the bell and until the librarian says I've got to go to class. I wait until Mr. Angelou flies in. Ha. Ha. Get it, flies in. Like an angel. Flies. I know I must be feeling a bit better if I can make a joke.

Christopher pulls at my shirt as I go to my seat. He looks at his desk when he whispers: "Can't play handball with you anymore, Jack. Paul can't either."

I swallow hard, but I understand. Maybe Christopher could stand up to George Hamel, but it's everyone else. Even nice guys. It is like they don't know I am Jack anymore. I'm the guy with the weird mother and no dad and the guy Mr. Angelou puts in detention and I'm just Butt Head. Butt Head. "That's okay, Christopher."

I eat my sandwiches running up the stairs to the library. You're not allowed to eat in the library. There are a few "Butt Heads" on the way, a few kicks, but it's all right. I try to forget what is outside. I find some books on cars and borrow one.

Last period. Swimming. "Get your sports bags," Mr. Angelou shouts as we head to the community pool next to the school. I have my suit on under my trousers so I can strip quickly at the side of the pool. "Ten laps freestyle." I've got to be first in the water. Make a fast getaway from the rest of the class. My head is like a lava pit as I dive into the water. The chlorine stings my eyes because I've forgotten my goggles, but the water and swimming are a relief.

Mr. Angelou watches like an eagle as we all splash in order up and down the chlorine water. I can't hear the kids. I go up and down, up and down by myself. I've got to think positive. I read that in the karate magazine. Positive. Don't think about Butt Head. Photographs. I'll think about photos. I am going to take some of Jack's Ponto. It is looking really interesting and Samantha has begged me to take some more photos of Puss. I want to do some of Nanna with Samantha and me. I'll have to do a time delay and leave the camera on the kitchen table then run and sit with Samantha and Nanna to be in the photograph. Sometimes a horrible feeling grips my stomach – that Nanna is going to die soon. I've told Mum that, but she said Nanna wouldn't leave us. Dad left though. Would Rob leave? I'm going to be sick.

"Dressing rooms," Mr. Angelou shouts. "You've got ten minutes." The showers. Should I go in first? Second? Last? Mr. Angelou's shouting at us to move it. "Hurry up." I head for the middle cubicle. The boys jam into the two other dressing cubicles and I can hear them throwing things and shouting. George Hamel's voice echoes against the walls. I can't help shuddering. Why do they hate me? I'm alone in the middle dressing room. My head's throbbing. I get changed as quickly as I can. Panic. Don't cry, Jack. Don't. Nearly dressed. A white blob catapults over the partition and slides down it. Another blob hits my back. I don't understand. Why? Why? Should I shout at them? Should I bang the wall? But there's only me in here. What will I do? There's jeering, "Butt Head," "Butt Head," then a hailstorm of spit and saliva. I can't move. I can't breathe. It's so filthy. So disgusting. A big one lands on my shoe, splattering like egg white. I stare at my shoe. Suddenly I grab my stuff and race out of the dressing rooms.

Nearly home. Samantha chatters. Anna walks quietly beside me. Mum blows a kiss from behind the supermarket window. Nearly home. Mr. Napoli waves. Mrs. Napoli gives me pistachio nuts for Mum. Nearly home. Up the stairs. One flight. Two flights. Three flights. I'm exhausted and only walk up one step at a time. Unlock the door. Mum's left afternoon tea out for us. Green apples and two donuts. Nanna phones with news about her specials. More socks and underpants. Puss rubs against my leg. Rob's car manual lies on the wobbly coffee table. Mum loves the wobbly coffee table and has put a piece of wood under the short leg so it doesn't wobble. Home.

Cramping eye spasms hammer my head. I bend over double with my hands around my head. Samantha drops her school bag. "Don't be sick, Jack. Don't be sick, Jack." She puts her arms around me.

I lie on Samantha's quilt in her bedroom. She brings me ginger ale. Puss curls up at the end of the bed. I close my eyes, but I'm not asleep. I listen to Samantha organize her things. Her music plays quietly, thin Ted is leaning against the bed, her colored pencils are

laid out carefully. I hear her pick up her pencils to sketch, color, draw and I feel safe. I doze off.

I wake up startled by Mum's call. "Dinner. Hot and delicious. Roast chicken." I hate that feeling of being woken up when I'm not ready. My mind is still half-asleep and woolly. No Rob. I'm glad he is not here tonight.

Mum carves the chicken. She gives me the leg and some white meat, peas, baked potato, pumpkin and fresh salad. My favorite, but not tonight. "I'm not hungry, Mum."

"Samantha told me. You've got a bad headache. Eat what you feel like, darling."

I nod while Mum pours some ginger ale for me.

"How was school?"

I want to tell Mum. I want to, but Samantha butts in and tells her all about her horrible sports teacher and her big project on pollution. I don't feel angry at Samantha for butting in. The wool in my head is starting to leave.

"And what happened at school for you, Jack?"

Mum's waiting. I touch my head trying to clear it. "Umm, I found a great book in the library on cars. Umm. I'm going to show Rob. Umm, the library is great. Umm. I'm going to look up some photographic books tomorrow at lunchtime."

"I'd like to talk to you about Rob." Mum hesitates. "Rob thinks you're both terrific kids. You both are. I don't know what I'd do without you." Mum tries to flatten her blond hair. "You've never had a real father. I'd like him to be your dad."

"Stepdad," I correct Mum.

"Well, yes."

I don't feel like thinking about my real father. I don't feel like talking about Rob. I don't feel like talking. I don't think I'm going to make it at school.

"Does that mean you'll be getting married, Mum?"

"Maybe, Samantha."

"Can I be the flower girl?"

Mum smiles. "Of course. You'll be the most beautiful flower girl in the world and you'll be ours.

"And what do you think, Jack?"

I blink hard. I love Mum so much and I even love Rob, but I don't know. We've worked things out so far. Mum, Samantha, me, with Nanna helping. Mum's waiting for my answer. I want my home to be the same. Home. A safe place. Different to school. I'm a kid, Mum. I don't know. "I want you to be happy, Mum, that's all."

The next few weeks at school are dangerous. Mr. Angelou is angry at me because I'm late to class every day. He says I'm missing too much work. But I have to be late otherwise George Hamel will get me. I've written so many lines — *I will not be late* — that the last time I had to do them Mr. Angelou said he would call in my parents. George Hamel shouted out, "Jack hasn't got a dad." Everyone laughed and Mr. Angelou told George Hamel off.

The library is fantastic. There is just the problem of getting up there as fast as I can. The other day a kid took a swipe at me with his cricket bat. Luckily, Mum hasn't noticed the bruise. The librarian likes me a lot and I help her to catalog books. I've discovered a fantastic book on agricultural experiments. My Jack's Ponto is sprouting the most amazing potato-onion shoots. Rob said I'm a genius. I'm not a genius at school, except at woodwork. My marks have gone down the toilet. I couldn't believe that I failed the last math test. I haven't told Mum. She thinks I'm going to be a scientist one day.

Christopher and Paul don't even say hello anymore. Too risky, but Anna does. She had a huge argument with a girl who called me "Butt

Head." Even the girls are calling me names now.

Mum writes me a note saying that I've got a headache so I won't have to go swimming. I walk to and from school now. "To get in shape," I tell Mum. She thinks that is fantastic. Samantha walks with me because she wants to get in shape too. She's been going to the gym with Mum every Sunday, while Rob and I do stuff together. Rob's fixing up his old bicycle for me. We got a new chain, but it's really hard to put on. I ask him about karate and he says he'll show me a few moves later.

Even Samantha has noticed that there is something wrong at school. Some of the kids in her class are telling her that I'm Butt Head. She told them that they were idiots. Samantha's not scared. What's wrong with me? I've got to talk to Mum, but she's so happy with Rob. No, no. I don't want to upset her. Rob won't understand. He'll think I'm weak and pathetic.

I've been practicing my karate. I know I could take George Hamel on now, but there are so many others. I don't know. I've nearly given up making jokes. I can't think of anything funny these days.

Friday afternoon at last. Anna is weird on the way home. "You know I wouldn't have done it if there was any other way."

"What are you talking about?"

"I'm your best friend, remember that."

Anna really is my best friend. "Do you want to go down to the beach tomorrow?"

Anna nods.

"Me too," Samantha says.

We climb up the three flights of stairs. Afternoon tea. Mum has left us a custard pie each. I don't feel like a custard pie and I love custard pies. We look up. Someone is opening the front door. "Nanna?" I call out.

No. It's Mum. She is still wearing her navy blue supermarket uniform. Her hair is pushed down by the supermarket cap, but bits of blond are sticking out of the sides. Samantha races up to hug her. Mum is never home early and she never comes in her supermarket uniform.

Rob arrives and he's in his work clothes. Gray trousers and a short-sleeved shirt. Rob never comes early and he never comes in his work clothes. Samantha runs into his arms and he swings her around. I half-call out, "Hi," then make a weak attempt at a joke. "We only need Nanna now."

Mum doesn't laugh. She always laughs even at my crummiest jokes. There's something in her eyes. They're watering and she's whispering. I can't understand what she's saying.

"Is something wrong, Mum?"

She stammers, "Anna told her parents everything. Everything. Mr. Napoli spoke to me, Jack. Mr. Napoli spoke to me, Jack. Mr. Napoli ..." Mum walks up to me and puts her arms around me and starts to cry quietly. "You're always so strong, Jack. You're only a boy, but you're so strong." Her hair is soft and the ends touch my face. I put my arms around her too. "I'm so sorry, Jack. I should have known. I should have. Too involved with myself." She holds me tighter and her crying becomes sobs, sobs that make her chest heave so that she can hardly breathe. I start crying too. Sobbing like Mum. It's like a flooding river. Rising sobs, overflowing the last months, drowning everything. Butt Head, escape into the library, spit on my back. Samantha snuggles next to me and then I feel Rob's hand on my shoulder.

There's no school today for me. There's no work today for Mum.

I hear Mum on the phone. "I want to speak to the principal."

Mum's hair is flying in all directions.

"Too busy, is he? I'm too busy too, but we're going to meet. I'll be in his office in half an hour."

Mum's face has gone splotchy.

"Are you saying half an hour isn't suitable? All right. When *is* suitable? In one hour? Two hours? Three hours? Or will I go directly to the Education Department?"

The voice on the other end of the phone gets loud.

"I WILL see the principal. I will see him NOW. I trusted your school with my Jack. I trusted your school, but it isn't safe." Mum's voice quivers. "Jack won't be coming back."

There's silence on the other line. Then a voice. A man's voice ...

Mum puts down the phone. "Jack. The principal will see us today at eleven o'clock."

I don't want to see the principal.

I can't believe Mum took time off from work. She has never done that before, even when we've been sick. Nanna would come over then with her cookies and specials. Mum is taking me out for lunch today. Just Mum and me. How great is that? Mum's wearing her long floral dress that kicks up when the wind catches the bottom. She's got a bright-yellow handmade sunflower in her hair. Mum looks beautiful.

Last night was incredible. Mum kept repeating how grateful she was to the Napolis. "Anna is your real friend, Jack." "Mr. and Mrs. Napoli are your real friends." "Anna didn't know what to do." "Mr. Napoli wanted to go the police." "Anna ... Mr. Napoli ... Mrs. Napoli ..."

Then Mum said something that made the throbbing inside my head stop. "Jack, you have to know ... paying off the mortgage, working, rushing to the shops, housekeeping, even my stupid gym mean nothing to me. It's all nothing, if I can't be there for you and Samantha."

She said she should have known there were real problems when my trousers were torn, or when I didn't make jokes, or when Christopher and Paul stopped coming over, or when I told her that I went to the library every lunchtime. "I was a library assistant. I've seen those kids who hide in the library because the playground is terrible. There are George Hamels out there, and stupid sheep who copy them. I should have seen it, Jack."

There was a lot of crying and Samantha sat right next to me on the couch. She lay her head against my shoulder. Rob kept saying he was going to the school and he would fix them. Mum held on to Rob's arm. "Thank you, Rob. I mean that. I do, but I'll go to the school with Jack. Just Jack and me."

Mum doesn't speak in the car as we drive to school. She's thinking and so am I. I don't want to go to see the principal. Everyone will know I've told on them. I'll be in even worse trouble than before. I'm scared. My head is a bubbling mess. Mum said the school has to do something. Mum said George Hamel has to be expelled. As if he'd be expelled. Mum said I can leave this school. I want to leave. I have to leave.

Usually Mum parks outside the gates, but not today. Mum drives right inside the schoolyard. "Jack. We're here." I feel sweat drip down my neck and molten lava roll through my head. I look at Mum who doesn't care that her hair is fluffed and that her yellow sunflower bobs around like in a field of wheat.

She stamps up the stairs, stamps along the corridor, stamps into the secretary's office with me tagging behind her. "I'm here to see the principal."

The secretary says quietly, "He's waiting."

The principal and Mr. Angelou stand up when we enter. "I hope you don't mind, but I've asked Mr. Angelou to join us. If there's a problem, we'll sort it out."

Mr. Angelou hates me. My throat dries up and I try to swallow. Mum sits down and I sit next to her. Mum said I could leave school. I want to leave NOW.

The principal adjusts his reading glasses as he flicks through the school report on his desk. "Jack's work has been deteriorating. We want to help Jack." The principal coughs. "But from what I understand from Mr. Angelou, he has been coming late to school and he hasn't been concentrating on his studies this term."

Mum listens while the principal rambles on about all the crimes I've committed – like being late, not participating in sports classes, failing to complete class work, absenteeism. When the principal finishes, he looks at Mum. Like a warrior, Mum faces them. Her colored dress is war paint and her sunflower is a headdress. "And whose fault is that?" Surprised, the principal jerks back a little. Mr. Angelou looks surprised as well. Mum doesn't give them time to answer. "Jack's bright. Really bright." I didn't know Mum thought that. Bright? "Do you know he's a photographer? That he fixes cars? He reads books? He discovers plants and seashells? Jack's responsible as well. I do double shifts at work because there's no dad, but it's all right because of Jack. He looks after his sister and cleans the house and fixes washers and tries to be grown-up. You don't know him, do you? Why don't you know my Jack? Why don't you care?"

The principal starts. "We want to know Jack." He takes off his glasses. "We do care."

"Did you ever find out why he's late to class? Why he can't go to sports? Why he isn't at school? Did you? Did you?"

The principal looks at Mr. Angelou.

"Well, you don't know Jack and you don't know what's happening in your own school." Mum's words target the principal and Mr. Angelou like arrows. Bull's eyes. Bull's eyes.

Mum tells them about me being pushed at the bus stop, escaping into the library, tagged as Butt Head, being shoved and kicked, being spat at over cubicle walls. "And the teachers are too busy to see. Don't want to see. Turn away. It's

easier to punish Jack, to show all those bullies that they're right. Jack is nobody." Mum's breathless and she puts her arms around me. "Jack's somebody. Jack's somebody and Jack won't be coming to this school again."

Mr. Angelou brings Mum a glass of water.

The principal waits for a while, then speaks to me. "Jack, we need to do some investigating. You are important to us. We will fix this, but you have to give us some time."

Time? I don't want to. I just want to leave.

The principal looks at Mum. "This school is here for Jack. Maybe it's a good idea that Jack has a few days off until we find out what's going on. Can we meet again? Say, two days."

Mum stares at me. I stare at the ground. My head is thunder.

Mr. Angelou's rosy cheeks glow and his bald head shines. He walks Mum and me to the door. "I promise we'll sort this out. Jack, you are somebody."

Somebody, Mr. Angelou said. I don't want to go back. Mum drives like she's got chewing gum on the wheels. The car jerks and shudders. She scrapes the side of the gutter as we turn the corner. Our old car is clunking furiously as we head towards the beach. Only when we see the sea, sparkling under the summer sun, does the car stop clunking. There is a parking spot and Mum swerves into it, squealing the tires.

The restaurant is expensive, overlooking the surf and sand. Mum asks for a table right at the window so we can look out. A waiter in a black shirt and trousers hands Mum a menu, then me. "Would you like something to drink while you look over the menu?"

I shake my head. Mum ignores me. "Yes, we'd like one pineapple juice and one watermelon and passion fruit juice. Both large, please." The waiter leaves and Mum takes my hand. "We're going to have a good time, Jack. Smile." I turn up the sides of my mouth. "What a pathetic smile." Mum makes a ridiculous face and I do smile.

Mum insists that I order a big T-bone steak, even though it costs too much. There are hot potato wedges with salad and tomatoes and mayonnaise sauce. Mum has salmon. The bread is hot and melts in your mouth. I feel better and have four slices. Mum has two.

We watch the surfers paddle out into the waves. I like bodysurfing. The main thing is not getting too worried about being dumped by a wave. Samantha hates being dumped and always ends up on the beach making a sandcastle, but Anna likes surfing.

"I've decided that I'm going to spend more time with you and Samantha. The mortgage is manageable these days, especially with Rob's help. Life can't be just about working."

The waiter arrives with two super-deluxe sundaes. Chocolate and lemon gelato swirl into a peak of nuts, hot chocolate sauce and pink marshmallows. Mum laughs. "Forget dieting forever."

"Nanna should be here. She'd love this."

"You're right, Jack. Next time we'll bring Nanna."

Sticky marshmallow slides deliciously down my throat. Mum gives me one of her marshmallows. I feel a bit better. A joke flashes into my mind.

"What do you get when you cross a marshmallow with a mouth?"

"What do you get, Jack?"

"Nothing. I've eaten it."

Mum laughs and I laugh. I don't know why we think it is so funny, but it is. Everything seems funny. When I point to a lady in a spotted bikini we laugh. Mum points to a man with a floppy hat. That makes us really laugh. When I point to a dog with a waggly tail, we just go hysterical.

Eventually we stop laughing, but we can't mention the waggly tail, otherwise we start again. Mum orders a cappuccino with lots of white froth and chocolate sprinkles. She lets me eat the froth and sprinkles. "Jack, we need to talk about a few things. School. Rob. Bullying ... You."

I don't want to talk. I can't think about those things right now.

"But not today. We need a rest."

Mum understands everything. After the restaurant, we take off our shoes and walk along the sand. Mum's sunflower looks golden. "Jack. It'll be all right."

I don't know if it will be all right. What I do know is that I have Mum and my family. Anna and Mr. and Mrs. Napoli are nearly family.

I wake up. No volcanoes. I'm NOT sick and I'm NOT going to school. Mum says Samantha has to go to school, which she thinks is unfair. But it's not. I have to do a whole list of things today. I am going to be very busy and Samantha wouldn't be useful. She'd just play around. Nanna is coming over. I have to admit that she's not very useful either, but she *thinks* she's a great help, which makes her happy.

My list of jobs:

1. Change the light bulb in Mum's side lamp. (Mum would live in the dark without me.)

2. Fix the armchair. (It's falling apart. I'll have to nail the arm on. It nearly came off when

Samantha jumped on it last week. I need my hammer for that.)

3. Hang up Samantha's new photograph of Puss in her bedroom. (It is an excellent character photo. Everyone says Puss looks so smug. She's lying in her favorite chair with her fur shining and her tail wrapped around her. There's this contented look on her face.) I'll need my drill.

4. Fill in the crack in the bathroom tile. (That's natural wear and tear. It's a grout job.)

After all that, I'm doing a photo shoot of Nanna and Jack's Ponto. I'm photographing every stage of the Ponto's development for scientific records. I'm also photographing Nanna just because she is Nanna. She is a good character to do. Her green eyes are interesting because they are never still. She's always investigating things, like what is in our fridge, or where is the plant she bought and it hasn't been watered, or who is doing karate because she's noticed my magazine. Her face is a lived-in face, with sun spots and lines and soft light hairs that sit on her top lip. But her cheeks are still pink and her eyes are like Samantha's. I want my face to be lived in when I'm old.

That is, if I ever get to be old with George

Hamel around.

Samantha grumps out the door and nearly falls over Puss. I call out goodbye to Mum and her from my bedroom window. Samantha gives a wave and Mum blows a kiss and does a twirl in her navy blue uniform. Right. Must get to work. Tools. Ah, everything is in order. On my birthdays and at Christmas I get another tool to add to my collection. Last Christmas Mum bought me my electric drill and Nanna bought the drill bits. I get nails, my excellent top-grade hammer, wood glue, and a chisel for fine work. The armchair is very broken. I turn it upside down, lay out my tools and get ready to begin when Nanna shuffles through the front door. Her face crinkles into a smile. "Jack, I'm just in time to help."

I roll my eyes. This means I'll be slower. She puts her specials on the kitchen table. Three chocolate bars, a loaf of whole-wheat bread and a T-shirt. "Come and try this on. I'll buy another one if it fits. It was half-price."

"Nanna. I'm busy."

"But I bought this for you. It'll only take a minute."

Sure. If I know Nanna, it'll take an hour because we'll have to discuss the T-shirt and if it fits, and if I like the color or do I want another color ... and we'll have to eat our chocolate bars and have a drink ... and Nanna will have to go to the bathroom because she says she's got a weak bladder ... and I'll have to tell her all about what I'm fixing.

I am right. I look at my watch. It's been an hour. Nanna sits on the couch so that she can get a good view of my work and give me advice.

"Jack, that's very good, but what about that bit sticking out of the leg." "Jack, be careful not to put glue on the carpet." "Jack, you need another nail there." "Jack, the other leg wobbles too." "Jack ..."

I'm going to kill Nanna. No, I had better not. I have a plan. I put on one of Samantha's quiet, boring songs. Then I hammer in time with the slow beat. It's warm in the family room because we get the morning sun. Nanna's head slowly bends forward. She lurches sideways for a second, then settles back into the couch. Nanna's asleep.

I like hammering and fixing with the music playing and Nanna quietly snoring on our old couch. I close Samantha's bedroom door when I drill the hole to hang Puss' picture. Nanna doesn't wake up.

I'm finished. I put my tools back in order and

then get my camera. Puss has curled herself right next to Nanna. Puss is a people cat. When I look at them through the camera lens, I feel this funny, warm feeling inside. Puss and Nanna look the same. Round and snuggled, with their whiskers drooping and their bodies moving in time with their breath. Puss' paw is on Nanna's lap and Nanna's hand is on Puss' stomach. I click.

Nanna wakes up for lunch. She loves her

food and afterwards we play cards until Samantha comes home with Anna. There is news from school.

I don't want Nanna to know about what has happened there. She'll get upset. Anyway, I am not going back to school. Mum said I didn't have to go back.

Anna is excited. "The principal called a school assembly in the hall. Mr. Angelou stood up and talked about bullying and 'how this school won't tolerate it.' He didn't mention Jack's name. Kids are going to get suspended for sure." Anna stamps her foot. "No one is allowed to push anyone around. No one will push you around anymore, Jack."

I roll my eyes. I don't believe that.

Nanna gets this worried look and the crinkles around her green eyes get tight and small. "Was Jack pushed around by other children?"

"No, no, Nanna. Anna's joking." I stare at Anna to be quiet, but she's not quiet.

"A substitute teacher is taking our class and Mr. Angelou isn't teaching us for the rest of the week. He's carrying out a huge investigation." She takes a breath before she gives the major news. "George Hamel wasn't in class all day. He's in serious trouble."

"Who is this George Hamel?" Nanna asks.

"He's the worst of the lot. He's always threatening kids." Anna pushes back her black curls. "Now he's the one who's scared." Anna looks at me.

I rub my prickly hair. I don't want to say anything. "That's good." I take out my camera and start clicking Anna.

"Don't do that, Jack." I click again. "Stop it. This is important. Aren't you happy?"

"Happy?" I click Samantha poking her tongue out at me. "I'm happy I could fix up all the things Mum wanted. I'm happy Nanna is here and you're here and Samantha." I put down the camera. "I'm happy Rob's coming over. He's taking me surfing." I tease a little bit. "I'm happy your dad was going to go to the police. It was crazy." I cough. "It was kind of nice that he wanted to do that."

Anna nods. "Dad does get emotional. People make fun of him because he's Italian. I don't like that, but he thinks it's funny. They wave their hands around and around and joke about him being a fruitologist."

"Like I did. You got angry with me, but it was only a joke."

Nanna's been listening, even though it is hard for her to catch all the words. She raises her finger to get our attention. "You have to laugh at yourself sometimes and the silliness of life. Anna, I like your father. He laughs because he knows it doesn't matter that he moves his hands around a lot. He's Italian, what can you expect?" Nanna smiles. "What's important to him is his family, you, a successful business."

"That's true."

"We've just got to understand jokes. What they mean. What they're used for. Sometimes people make jokes that hurt. They're not meant to be funny. Some jokes blame people for problems, some make them into scapegoats." Nanna puts her hand over mine. "You'd never do that, would you, Jack?"

"No." I can't tell Nanna that I was called Butt Head. It would hurt her.

Rob's come early. He decided we are all going to the beach for surfing, swimming and fish and chips on the grass slope above the beach. "Nanna can come, and Anna. Ask your parents, Anna, and get your bathing suit."

Everything's packed up by the time Mum opens the door. The car is loaded with towels, pails and shovels, picnic chairs, a folding table and a beach ball. "Get your suit on," we all shout at Mum.

We're off to the beach. Rob and I head for

the surf. Anna and Samantha are collecting shells for the sandcastle. When I look back at Mum and Nanna, they're talking.

"Surf's up," Rob shouts as he dives into a wave. I dive in after him.

Mr. Angelou has phoned. We've got a meeting with him this afternoon. Mum is leaving work early. The manager of the supermarket said it was all right. He has cut Mum's hours down so that she is not doing any extra shifts, or Saturdays. She is talking about going back to work in the library. She'd like that.

I get this awful feeling walking into the school. As we pass the classroom windows, I see kids at their desks. Christopher looks out. That is not going to be me. Mum promised. I don't have to come back. Mum has got a serious look on her face. She is wearing her serious cream blouse and her serious maroon cotton skirt. Well, the skirt is nearly serious, except for a huge white daisy printed on the front and two smaller daisies printed on the back.

Mr. Angelou looks even taller and rounder than usual when he stands up. He walks towards us with his hand extended. He shakes Mum's hand, then mine. It's a strong, safe handshake. "Please take a seat."

He sits down too, bends his head for a moment. His bald spot glows. Mr. Angelou presses his hands together, then speaks to me. "I've done a lot of investigating in the past two days. The librarian mentioned you to me before. She was worried. I should have listened more seriously to her. Jack, you're not the only one." He coughs. "I pride myself on being a good teacher. I'm an executive teacher as well as your classroom teacher. Jack, I feel partially responsible."

Is this Mr. Angelou? He's given me so many lines to write that I used to think my hand would fall off.

"I'm aware of some of the incidents now. I've talked to every student in your year." He pauses to think. "Looking back, I remember you tried to ask me for help. I remember seeing and hearing things that I should have followed up." His forehead creases into lines. "Being too busy is no excuse."

My head thuds. I remember trying to tell Mr. Angelou that it wasn't me. It was George Hamel who pushed me off my chair in class. I wanted to tell Mr. Angelou why I didn't want to go into the locker room, why I was late, why my school trousers were torn, why I missed school, why I didn't answer any questions in class … I couldn't. I feel breathless. It really hurt when they called Mum names. When they said my father left because of me. And I just took it, like a coward.

"Teachers are busy, think someone else will handle it, make excuses." Mr. Angelou looks at Mum. "But we hear you now. This school, and the school community – the principal, staff, parents and students – will deal with it. I promise you." Mr. Angelou takes out a large handkerchief and wipes his lined forehead.

"It's been terrible," Mum stammers. She reaches for my hand. "Jack has been so brave. He didn't want to worry me. Imagine having the courage to get up every day to go to a place where you know you have to run and hide, get beaten up, spat at." Mum's crying and I hold her hand tightly. "I don't think I could have made it. Jack's a braver person than me."

"And me. I'm going to ask Jack something important. Something I don't know if I could do. Jack," he hesitates, "I'm asking you to do this, so that other students don't have to go through what you have."

I feel nervous.

"It's an enormous thing to ask. As a school community we are putting in an anti-bullying program because of you and others who have been bullied." He takes a breath. "Bullies shouldn't be given the power to make you leave this school. I'm asking you to stay and fight, for a while at least. And if, after that, you do decide to leave, it's because you want to, not because you're running away."

"Run away?" I look at Mum. That's what I want to do.

"If you run, you'll always be afraid and there are other bullies out there. I know you deserve more."

I look down at my hands. This is too hard.

"You won't be alone. I'll be there and we'll fight this together. It won't be easy and you won't win overnight. It'll be a long, tough road, but I promise you that you'll win. I promise you."

Mum speaks quietly. "Darling, I will do whatever you decide. If you want to leave this school, that's all right. If you want to stay and fight, that's all right. Whatever you choose, I'm here for you."

There is silence. I keep looking at my hands. Samantha and Anna are at this school. I want to walk home with them. It's easier for Mum if I stay. There's the editing room. I work on my photos there. Other schools might not have that. George Hamel ... I shudder. I don't want him to win. I don't want people like that to win. Stay here? Can I take it? But I don't want to be afraid anymore. I look at Mr. Angelou whose bald head is shining in the sunlight. "Maybe. I suppose."

He shakes my hand again. A strong handshake. "I'll see you Monday before school in my office. I have a plan."

I sort of smile. Mr. Angelou has a plan.

Saturday. An important excursion. We are all going to visit Grandad in the cemetery, except for Rob. He's working. I take my camera. Nanna says we need to talk to Grandad. Mum's packed a picnic lunch. Samantha's put on her rainbow dress, which is nearly the same as Mum's, and a yellow straw sun hat. Mum has her yellow straw sun hat on too. Oh no, Nanna's arrived and guess what? She's wearing a yellow straw sun hat. She bought all the hats on special from Susie's Splendid Discount Store. Actually, she bought one for Anna too. She's coming with us. I wonder if she is wearing hers as well. I stick my head out of my bedroom window. Guess what? Anna's waiting outside and, yes, you guessed it. She's wearing her yellow straw sun hat.

Nanna is very happy as she sits in the front seat of the car in her yellow straw sun hat, with all the other yellow straw sun hats. "That was a very good buy, wasn't it? Everyone loves these hats. Maybe I should have bought more?" Samantha starts giggling, then Anna, then Mum, then me, then Nanna. All you can see is a mass of bouncing yellow straw sun hats and a yellow baseball cap Nanna bought for me.

The cemetery is on a hill that looks out over the bay. We drive through heavy, wrought-iron gates into the cemetery. There are rows and rows of plots. Some are magnificent with huge old sandstone monuments. Others are simple, with gravel on the flat top bit and a small headstone. There are mausoleums that house whole generations of families. I love the marble angels and doves. On some plots there are wooden crosses, or Jewish stars, or other symbols, or sometimes nothing, depending on people's religion. We drive right to the top of the city of stone where Grandad lives.

Nanna and Grandad chose this place. It fits four people. Grandad is the only one there.

Nanna will go there one day and probably Mum. So there won't be room for both Samantha and me. I bet I get left out. Mum told me not to worry about it because we won't be going there for ages. She said she'll work it out that we are all together. Anyway, it is beautiful up here. Grandad always has a view of the sea with the waves rolling onto the sand and fishing boats. He loves the sea. Maybe that's why I love the sea too. I take some photographs.

Nanna doesn't shuffle towards Grandad's plot. She walks like she's young again. Taking out her garden clippers, she begins to trim the potted rose bush. We help with the weeding and sweep the granite top. "That looks better," Nanna says. Being with Grandad makes her different. She's not old here. "We can have our picnic now."

Mum brings out a folding chair for Nanna and throws a blanket over the path next to Grandad for us. Grandad always liked a picnic and Mum has brought his favorite foods – cheese, fresh bread, pickles, olives, cashews and apples. Grandad had excellent teeth and always enjoyed a crispy apple. Poor Nanna can't eat crispy red apples. Mr. Napoli gave Anna a whole bag of crispy red apples for the picnic.

There is a cool breeze from the bay and

Samantha's hat blows off. We chase it right down the hill. Nanna gets worried because they've sold out of yellow straw sun hats at Susie's Splendid Discount Store. "I know I can't get any more," she says, and her green eyes squint in the sun as they follow the path of the yellow straw sun hat. Luckily, I grab it just before it flies over the fence.

"Be careful with your hat," Mum says as she ties the hat's ribbon under Samantha's chin.

It is time to talk to Grandad. Anna understands about that. I think it is because she's Italian or maybe because the Napolis love their family. "Your family does not die. They are always part of your life," Mr. Napoli says.

Samantha tells Grandad about Puss. Anna doesn't know Grandad, but she tells him about her grandfather who was a farmer. "He grew olive trees."

"Grandad loved olives," Nanna says. She waits, then looks at me. "Grandad loved us. He loved you especially, Jack." She catches her breath, then sits up straight. "You know you're never alone when you have people who love you."

Nanna reaches out for my hand. "Jack, you forgot. You're not alone."

She touches Grandad's grave. "Jack, you have

to promise, right here in front of Grandad, that you won't forget that. If you get into trouble, you will ask for help from us. There's no excuse, no reason that you can't. Otherwise, we feel like we've failed you, Jack. You don't want us to feel bad, do you?"

I shake my head.

"You have to promise to let us be there for you. Promise, Jack."

Promises. There are two promises now. Mr. Angelou's promise. Mine. "I promise."

We sit looking out at the sea. Samantha plays chase with Anna. Nanna rests her head against Grandad's grave. Mum takes off her yellow straw sun hat and lets the wind blow her blond hair into a tangle.

Before we pack up our picnic basket, I take out my camera. Everyone has to put on their yellow straw sun hats for my photographs. Mum puts her arms around Nanna. Click. Samantha and Anna stick out their tongues. Click. Mum swirls around. Click. They all hold hands. Click. I put the camera on Grandad's granite top and run to get into the photo. Click.

Sunday is work. Mum decides that we have to do a total cleaning of the house. "The kitchen today. It's the beginning of the new us," Mum announces as she empties the cupboards. Samantha's helping Mum stack the wanted and unwanted piles on the table.

"Samantha, don't throw that out, my favorite egg cup." It's a blue hippopotamus with a hole in its head – that's for the egg. "Nanna gave that to me when I was three."

"When was the last time you used it? Never. And its ear is broken off."

"Right then, and when your ear is broken off we'll throw you out." I grab my hippopotamus. "I'm going to stay here and watch you, otherwise you'll throw out important things."

Mum's hair is in a frizz. "Stop arguing. Jack, nothing will be thrown out before you check the pile. You're supposed to go with Rob and pick up the new cupboards." Mum finally decided to change the color from orange to cream. It was a huge decision for her, even though she has been complaining about the orange doors for as long as I can remember. It costs a lot of money, but Mum said it has to be done. It is like she is getting rid of past stuff and making room for Rob.

"I said GO. Rob's waiting."

"Come on, Jack," Rob calls. "Phew. We're lucky to get out of there." He winks. "Guys are great escape artists."

I jump the last six steps down the stairs easily. I am getting good at it. Rob checks the trailer that he has hitched onto the car. We drive slowly to the hardware store.

Rob's wrong. Guys aren't great escape artists. Carrying the cupboards up three flights of stairs is really exhausting. Halfway, we have to sit down and have a drink.

That was lucky for Samantha and Mum who are taking ages to sort out the kitchen.

Eventually they finish and head for Mum's bedroom.

I get my tools and Rob gets his and we take control of the kitchen. It is serious work changing the cupboards: drilling holes, hammering in wall plugs, screwing in doors. We carry piles of orange laminate out of the kitchen and store it the family room. Rob and I are a good team.

"So how's school?"

Rob knows how school is. Mum tells him everything without even asking me if it's all right. I don't like that. "Better."

"I hear you're staying on."

"That's right. For a while."

I hold a cupboard while Rob pushes it into place. Sweat is dripping down his back. He turns to look at me just for a second. "You know, I'll give you a hand. Teach you a bit of karate. Back you up at school. If anyone gives you a hard time, tell them you've got a step-dad."

Stepdad? A funny feeling vibrates along my spine. "I'm all right."

"I know you are, Jack. Just remember I'm here."

We're dead tired by Sunday evening, but the kitchen is clean, organized, cream and Mission

Brown, and finished. Samantha puts on some music. We listen to dance music while we eat pizza sitting on piles of orange laminate. "Can't wait to throw all this orange out," Mum says. "I can't believe it's finally going. You were all fantastic. Fantastic." Mum hums in time with the music.

"Mum. The big closet near your dressing table is empty." Even though Samantha's asking Mum the question, she's looking at Rob. "Will Rob be moving in full time, Mum?"

Samantha has such a big mouth. We're all happy. Why is she bringing this up? She wants Rob to live here just because he spoils her. She is so greedy.

Things are fine the way they are.

"When we're all ready, Samantha."

Nanna arrives with chocolate ice cream. She wants to see the new cupboards. Nanna approves and Mum doesn't even care that Nanna brought chocolate ice cream. She says we've all worked so hard we deserve ice cream. I have two helpings. Suddenly Mum jumps up. "I feel great. Terrific music." She takes Samantha's hand and they start dancing around the family room until Nanna's tapping her feet and deciding to join in. Nanna is hopeless and shuffles from one foot to the other. Rob won't dance, but says he likes watching. Me too, but Nanna needs a partner. So I jump up and dance too. We go to bed really late.

Groan. Monday morning. I have to get up. I drag myself out of bed. There's the usual routine, except our family room looks like a building site and our kitchen is cream. Mum is rushing. Samantha is going to school with Anna later. I have to go early.

Rob wants to drive me to school. I don't feel like talking in the car. Why did I agree to go back? Am I crazy? We pull up at school. "Just wait," Rob says as he parks the car. He gets out and looks around. Boys are hanging around the front gates. Rob puts his arm on my shoulder, then does a karate chop in the air. "We're going through the front gates, Jack."

Rob strides towards the gates. "Jack, you look them in the eye."

We walk through those gates. A boy sneers, laughing. "Hey, haven't seen you for a while, Jack."

Rob stops. Turns around to the boy. He puts his arm on the boy's shoulder. "Hey, what'd you say?"

The boy doesn't answer.

"What did you say?" Rob's voice is rough.

"Nothing," he whimpers.

"Right, then." Rob stares him in the eye and so do I.

Mr. Angelou is in his office. He's waiting for

us. Rob introduces himself, but doesn't say much. Mr. Angelou and Rob shake hands, like making a pact. "If you need me, call." Then Rob leaves and it is just Mr. Angelou and me.

Mr. Angelou opens his drawer and pulls out two colas. He gives me one. We open the tops of the cans at the same time and they hiss together. "We're going to win this one."

Mr. Angelou starts talking about photography. How does he know it's one of my favorite subjects? He says that this afternoon, instead of going to class, I can work on my photos. He's interested in my photography. I'm going to work on the photos of Mum, Nanna, Samantha and Anna in their sun hats. I'm thinking of making the picture really bright with streams of light coming from all angles. There are some great shots of Nanna resting on Grandad's grave too. I want to capture her green eyes. I know Nanna's really old, but her eyes seem to know a lot.

Mr. Angelou thinks I should enter the Inter-School Photographic Competition.

I feel good. It's hard to explain why I start telling Mr. Angelou things after that, things I've never told anyone else. Private, private things about having no dad, worrying about Mum and Samantha and Nanna, being scared we would have no money, scared that Rob will be like my dad. Mr. Angelou gives me another cola. Then takes one for himself.

He drinks nearly the whole can before talking again. Mr. Angelou tells me that he has spoken to every student, every class. "There will be no exception, no excuse. Anyone who calls you Butt Head or even hints at bullying you, or any other student, will be pulled out of class and their parents phoned. If there's no satisfactory excuse, the student will be suspended. Even expelled." His rosy cheeks go redder. "I'm putting the pressure on and I'll keep it on. If a teacher, another student, a parent, you, report bullying, I'll act." He pauses. "But it won't be enough in the end. What I'm doing now is only creating a level playing field for a while. Do you understand, Jack?"

"Yes." I try to joke. "The field is bumpy now, isn't it?"

Mr. Angelou nods. "Yes. Too bumpy. Bullies like George Hamel use their power to feel good about themselves. When others follow them, bullies get strong. Well, they're not." He waits. "Take away their supporters, make them stand alone and they're weak." He finishes his cola. "Bullies find what they think are weaknesses in another person and then attack."

He looks at me. "Like having a single mother."

I jerk forward. "She's a great mum. The best, and lots of kids have single mothers."

"That's true, Jack. But bullies pick on the differences. They pick on anything – if you're fat or have freckles or can't play sports or you're poor or rich. They start the name-calling. Fatso. Pimple Face. Dumbo. Butt Head. A name can be funny at first, but by repeating it again and again, it becomes a weapon. If you're not confident, it becomes an even stronger weapon. When enough people say the name and say it loudly enough, people start to forget who the person really is. You become Fatso, Pimple Face or Butt Head."

I feel like choking. I remember running up the library stairs. Christopher not playing ball with me. How kids who would say hello before, nice kinds of kids, just stopped. "Why did they hate me so much, Mr. Angelou? What did I do to them? Why did they want to kick me and call me names and spit at me?"

"They couldn't see you anymore, Jack. You were Butt Head." He presses his lips together. "But not anymore." He looks at me. "You can stop it. You can make them see Jack again."

"I don't know how, Mr. Angelou."

"At home you're Jack, aren't you?"

I nod.

"You're a photographer. You tell great jokes. Your mum tells me you help her a lot. Rob says you're clever with your hands. That's Jack. It's a great Jack. You've got to believe that."

I shrug.

"And you have something George Hamel doesn't have."

I look up at Mr. Angelou.

"Your family. That's what you have."

Mr. Angelou stands up. "We're going to meet every morning before school to talk." He looks at me. "Jack, you're a good kid. We'll do this."

Together, we walk to class.

I like the morning talks with Mr. Angelou, but it is still dangerous out there. Last week two boys blocked the stairwell and I had to push past. Christopher saw it and ran up behind me. Then Paul followed. We all pushed past.

Mr. Angelou talks to George Hamel too. "I want to find out why he's like what he is," he tells me. "George Hamel needs some help, Jack." I shudder. George Hamel and his gang still walk around like thugs. I avoid them. There are kids I play with again. They're all right.

"Come on, Jack," Christopher shouts at me. "Handball."

The competition is fierce. Paul gets out right away. Five other guys are banging the ball against the wall. "Out." "Out." "Out." In the end it is Christopher and me. He beats me. I warn him. "Next time, I'll get you."

George Hamel and his gang aren't in the schoolyard at lunchtime anymore. They eat their lunch outside the teachers' room or with Mr. Angelou.

Christopher is explaining the new spin he's developed on the ball, when a couple of kids call out Butt Head.

I look at them right in the eye, but before I say anything, Christopher jeers, "It's better than being a Butt Wiper, you losers." Paul is laughing at them and so am I. Christopher looks around and sees the supervising teacher. "Right, let's report you jerks." They race off as Christopher heads towards the teacher with us behind him.

"Don't bother reporting them, Christopher."

Christopher turns around. "Jack, I feel bad about what happened." He kicks the grass. "I should have stood up for you. Sorry." Christopher walks towards the teacher.

School posters are everywhere. Tacked onto classroom doors, in the hall, even on the bathroom wall.

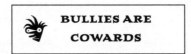

BULLIES ARE COWARDS

> **WHAT'S THE DIFFERENCE BETWEEN THE FLU AND A BULLY?**
>
> **THE FLU MAKES YOU SICK THE BULLY IS SICK**

> **BULLIES ARE WEAK**
>
> **NO BULL !!!!!!!!!!**

Rob has moved in. We hardly noticed at first. It's just that the four days he would come over became five days and then all week, every week. Mum gets mad when he leaves his shoes and socks in the family room. She says he is encouraging me to do the same. I don't, except when I have to leave them at the entrance. I need to put them on fast when I play basketball with Christopher out back, or meet Anna to go to the beach, or help Nanna with her specials. Rob is teaching me karate. Since Rob has moved in, he drops me early at school every day. "Is everything all right?" he always asks.

"Fine, Rob."

Mr. Angelou's smiling when I come in this

morning. He holds up my last math test. "Big improvement, Jack."

"Must be your teaching."

Mr. Angelou laughs. "You're right." Then he's serious. "George Hamel isn't as lucky as you. He finds schoolwork hard. He's started remedial lessons at lunchtime."

Am I supposed to care? What does Mr. Angelou want me to say? I'm just glad he isn't in the playground at lunch. "That's good for George Hamel," but more importantly, "Mum's gotten the job at the library."

"Are you happy about that?"

"Yes," except I'll miss waving to her through the supermarket window on the way home. "She'll love not wearing a uniform."

Mr. Angelou rubs the top of his bald head. "Your mother looks like summer."

I like that. Mum does look like summer with her blond hair and her floral dresses and bright colors. Everything she does is summer, even her cooking. She's cooking the best dinners these days. Experimental cooking, she calls it. Rob calls it experimental indigestion.

In the mornings, Mr. Angelou and I talk about all sorts of things. Sports, Rob, school, Samantha, articles in the newspapers, kids drinking alcohol, just anything. It makes George

Hamel seem stupid. It makes the kids who followed him seem like that too. It makes me wonder why I let them bully me.

I'm seriously working on my photographic collection for the Inter-School Competition. I show Mr. Angelou. He's very impressed with it. When I showed Samantha and Anna yesterday afternoon, they were impressed too. "I love that one with everyone in the yellow straw sun hats," Anna said, pushing away her black curls from her face. Her hair is getting curlier and she hates it. I think she looks great.

Samantha kept studying the one where Nanna is superimposed over the grave. "She looks like she's flying. It's amazing, Jack." She made me laugh when she said, "You're so smart, Jack."

She usually doesn't say that, especially when I bother her. Mainly she calls me an idiot, a pain, and irritating.

Mr. Angelou wants me to work in a special group this morning in the meeting room next to his office. It's the assignment on Egypt. "Get your books, paper and pen and I'll see you there."

Kids are racing into classrooms. Paul hits my arm as he runs past. I shove him back just before he's out of reach. "Get you back later,"

Paul calls out, laughing, as he disappears into the classroom.

"Right, as if," I call back. Paul's getting better at handball. He nearly beat me the other day.

Mum borrowed a terrific book on pyramids. Luckily I've got it here. Better get moving. Through the window, it looks like there are only about five kids in the room. Two girls. Three guys. I open the door. George Hamel looks up. This sinking feeling hits my stomach like a rock. I squint like Nanna does when she's concentrating. Right, I'm not scared of George Hamel. Not after everything that has happened. What can George Hamel do to me? Nothing. Well, he could break my arm. I heard he did that to someone at rugby the other day. I grit my teeth. I nod at George Hamel, then look around. There is Bill. He plays handball at lunchtime.

The girls are too busy talking to notice me. There are a few grunts from the boys. George Hamel smirks. I take a desk. Mr. Angelou walks in. "Is everyone ready? I want two groups." Mr. Angelou points to George Hamel. "You're over there with Jack and Bill." What's wrong with Mr. Angelou? This is George Hamel, Mr. Angelou. George Hamel stands up. It is amazing. He has got to be at least six feet and that is only the size of his head. I smile at my joke. I must be feeling better. Then I look at George Hamel again. No, I don't feel better.

"I want the first section of the assignment to be completed this morning." Mr. Angelou is tough. Everyone knows he is tough. "There'll be detentions if the work isn't done."

The pyramids. I open my book, look at my watch. George Hamel is still sneering at me. I take a deep breath and look him in the eye. "Let's get started." Bill starts to sketch the Great Pyramid of Cheops. He's drawing a pyramid shape before he starts on the internal passages leading to the tomb. I note the important sections in my book. *The Great Pyramid is 450 feet high.* Huge. George Hamel is looking at my book.

"Imagine all those people carrying those gigantic blocks of sandstone to build them," I say. "A lot of people died building those pyramids. It was dead hard. DEAD hard."

Bill laughs. George Hamel grunts. "Dead hard? Yeah, it was only meant for dead people."

I roll my eyes. Bill does too. George Hamel has no sense of humor. "*When the Pharaoh died, he took living people with him. His servants, wives, advisors.*" I shudder. "His tomb was right at the

bottom of the pyramid, under all those huge stones. Then the pyramid was sealed shut. No one could get out. They'd have starved there. Suffocated. In the dark. Right at the bottom." I think of Grandad's grave in the sunlight, overlooking the bay with Nanna visiting.

The sketches are finished. "They are great," I say, but George Hamel doesn't sketch anything. George Hamel doesn't have much to say. George Hamel can't write very well. He can't write. I never knew that before. Imagine that? How can you do your assignments or answer questions or be at school if you can't write? I look at his huge head and orange hair. He's got this expression on his face that looks tough, but his big hands just lie on the desk like pieces of blubber. He can't write.

When Mr. Angelou comes back to check the assignment, I give him our work. "How did everything go?"

"It was okay."

"Was it?" He glances at George Hamel.

"Yes." I can't believe it, but I feel sorry for George Hamel.

Mr. Angelou's bald head gleams. "I'll see you all this afternoon at gym." He looks at me. "Jack, that means you too."

Mum's swirling around like poppies in a storm. Her face is red and her dress is red except for white petals along the edges and on the sleeves. There's a silk poppy in her hair. Her hair is a fuzz ball.

Nanna's shuffling through the door with a load of green specials: broccoli, cabbage, string beans, peas in pods. "Please, not now," Mum tells her. I can see Nanna's feelings are hurt and I take her green specials to the kitchen. Nanna feels better.

Rob's got black grease on his shoes from work. "I left work early today and I didn't notice," he explains, but Mum's already rubbing the carpet clean. He starts taking his shoes off. The flower in Mum's hair bobs up and down as she rubs. "Don't you dare leave your shoes in the family room."

"I wouldn't do that, Poppy." He smiles, looking at me. Mum is suspicious that he's laughing at her, but she doesn't answer because Samantha arrives with her hair in the weirdest shape. "Mum, can you help?"

Mum starts giggling. That puts Samantha in a bad mood. "I don't want your help if you laugh at me, Mum."

Mum has to beg Samantha's forgiveness because no one wants Samantha in a bad mood. She gets so grumpy. "Sorry, sorry." Mum kisses Samantha so much that Samantha starts giggling.

"You're tickling me, Mum."

Mum runs for a brush. She brushes Samantha's hair into a ponytail and puts a gold ribbon through it. Samantha smiles and even I have to admit she does look beautiful.

Anna arrives. She looks beautiful too. She's finally worked out what to do with her curly black hair. A silver headband pushes her hair back, like a waterfall.

Mum's in a panic because this is the afternoon of the photographic exhibition. Dinner is already made for tonight, the house is tidy, Puss has been fed, the table set, everyone is dressed.

Samantha and I have been helping all day. I say to Rob, "Mum doesn't GET it. It's my exhibition."

He winks. "It's hers too."

Anna and I escape into my room. I close the door and see Anna shaking her head. "This room is a mess."

"It may be a mess to you, but it's vacuumed, cleaned and dust-free. Mum forced me to do it. Anyway, I know where everything is and my tools and books are perfect."

"Car manuals. How interesting. Yes, they are perfect." She looks out of the window at the Napolis' Super Delicioso Fruitologist Market. Her mother is stacking oranges at the front and you can just see her father at the cash register. "Mum and Dad wanted to come to the exhibition, but there wasn't anyone to run the shop. They'll be over for dinner."

I lean against the sill next to Anna and look out. There is a breeze and the smell of hot bread wafts through the window. We talk about our favorite breads and the delicious cookies made in the bakery.

"I'm so glad that your photos were chosen for the Inter-School Exhibition."

"The photography teacher helped me, and Mr. Angelou did as well. I had to redo the editing heaps of times to get the effects I wanted."

"'Sunlight at the Grave' is a wonderful title. Your Nanna looks gentle and peaceful in those photos."

"Nanna's a fantastic subject. So are you, Anna."

She smiles. "That day at your grandad's grave was special. You caught a feeling that was more than just taking pictures." Anna thinks for a while. "The photos were about family, and me, of course. I'm nearly family. About being together, talking, sharing. It's hard to explain."

I nod because it is hard to explain.

"I'm glad the photographs are in the exhibition. Not everyone will be able to see what's really in them, but we can see." She furrows her eyebrows. "Everything's all right now, isn't it?"

The bullying seems ages ago now. I think about it for a while. "Some kids still call me names when there's no teacher around, but not many anymore. I tell them off or laugh when they do. George Hamel leaves me alone. I've got a few friends, and the teachers are better." I rub my hand over my hair. It's getting longer. "It's all right."

Anna nods.

"Time to go," Mum calls out. Insanity hits as we pile out the door. Nanna nearly trips on the top step, but luckily Rob catches her. Mum's poppy falls out and there is a desperate search for it. The poppy is behind the door. Samantha jumps four steps and she knows she can't do that yet. She grazes her knee and Mum and Anna comfort her. I have to race back upstairs and get a band-aid.

Rob gets mad. Rob doesn't get mad often. His hair is standing up. He's shouting, "STOP!" We look at him and he shouts again. "Everyone, don't move. Don't move!"

No one does move because we're all amazed that he's shouting.

He takes Mum's arm, opens the car door to the front seat. "Get in." Mum does. He holds Samantha's hand and sits her next to Mum. Then he helps Nanna into the back seat. Anna and I follow. "Put your seat belts on." We all do. Rob switches on the radio. Samantha snuggles between Rob and Mum. "Can you put it on my channel, Dad?" Rob rubs Samantha's hand for a second, then presses the button for Samantha's radio station. I feel strange when Samantha calls Rob, Dad. But he is like a dad to us now.

The exhibition isn't at school. It is in the local library. I feel nervous as Rob drives into the parking lot. "Calm, everyone," Rob says as we get out of the car. He holds Mum's hand. Nanna holds Samantha's hand. Anna and I walk into the library together. There are a lot of people I don't recognize from other schools. A few kids I know say hello. Kids who used to call me Butt Head come up and say my photos are great. I get this weird feeling when they do that.

Large stands covered in black linen are placed throughout the library foyer. Framed photographs with titles printed in black ink hang on both sides of the stands. The name of the photographer is right at the top. Mum takes a catalog.

"Let's go and find Jack's," Nanna says. She pulls at the elastic in her underpants. I bet she's wearing her purple ones. I don't wear my purple underpants because they itch. Samantha and Mum agree. Itchy purple underpants. What's wrong with me? Why am I thinking about itchy purple underpants? I must be nervous.

Samantha calls out really embarrassingly, "They're here. Over here."

Luckily Rob holds Mum's hand tightly so that she doesn't run over and make a spectacle of herself. Except I don't care if she does make a scene. Mum's face is nearly all smile. I've made her proud of me. My head doesn't hurt. Nothing hurts. I stand between Mum and Nanna. Nanna has tears in her eyes. "Grandad is in these pictures. He's proud of you, like I am." I get this lump in my throat. Mum and Nanna and even Grandad, are proud of me.

My school librarian especially finds me to say how impressed she is with my photos. Mr. Angelou strides up to us. "Well done." He chats a while before going to speak to other parents and kids. Mr. Angelou is coming for dinner tonight.

The chief librarian taps the microphone to get everyone's attention. There are going to be speeches on the podium. The chief librarian says how proud he is that the library could be involved in this exhibition. The school inspector says how proud he is of all the schools and the entrants involved and how grateful he is for the library's support. Every principal thanks the inspector, the library, teachers, students. The judges talk about the entries ... and Samantha yawns. Mum's dropped her poppy somewhere on the floor, which is a lucky excuse for Samantha to go poppy hunting. Nanna stands right next to me smiling, but I know she can't hear most of what's said. Maybe that's good.

My feet are getting sore standing here. I see

orange juice on the refreshment table. I'm hot. I jump when Mum squeezes my arm. What? What? Names are being called out. The inspector is shaking the hand of every photographer and handing him a certificate and a book. My name's called. I can't move. "Go on." Anna shoves me forward. The crowd parts as I walk towards the podium. "Congratulations," the inspector says. When the inspector hands me my certificate there's this awful clapping from the back. It's Nanna, Mum, Samantha (who has found Mum's poppy) and Rob. They are so loud. Then I look at the front. There's another loud clapper. Mr. Angelou.

The local newspaper takes photographs of all entrants and asks questions about everyone's photos. Then we have permission to eat. Mum says not to eat too much at the library because she has made a big dinner at home. There are sandwiches, cream cakes and cookies there. Nanna eats five cookies. I look at Mum. Nanna doesn't care about dinner. I only have two cookies, one apple pie and two orange juices. I'm so thirsty. I might have another orange juice.

When we get home, Mr. and Mrs. Napoli are waiting for us outside our building. Mr. Napoli is holding up a huge bunch of yellow carnations for Mum. He hugs Mum, Nanna, then Rob. Rob goes all stiff and uncomfortable, which makes Mum laugh. "Rob, don't worry, he's Italian." Mrs. Napoli hugs everyone too.

As we open the front door, there are delicious smells of roast chicken and baked potatoes. Everyone wants to look at my prize, even Puss who walks over the cover of the book, *Magic Moments in Photography*. It's a great book. Nanna looks at the pictures and says my photos are better than the book's. I'd expect Nanna to say that. I'm always the best to her.

Mr. Angelou arrives with a bottle of wine and chocolates. So we're all here. Mum doesn't want any help in the kitchen while she's doing last-minute preparations. Rob's pouring drinks. Samantha's patting Puss, and sitting next to Nanna repeating anything interesting that someone says. Nanna's hearing gets worse when a lot of people are talking at the same time. I'm showing Mr. Angelou my book.

"This is a great achievement, Jack." Mr. Angelou flips over the pages. Then he stops and looks at me. "If you believe in yourself you can do anything."

"You mean I can fly to Jupiter?"

He winks before turning to Mr. Napoli who wants his attention. Mr. Napoli is describing his renovations at the Napolis' Super Delicioso

Fruitologist Market. He talks a lot about those renovations. When he is finished, Mr. Angelou smiles at me and puts out his hand. "Shake, Jack. You know, we won." I shake his hand. He smiles. "YOU won, Jack."

Samantha runs to turn on the music. It's announcement music. Mum comes through the open door into the family room. She is carrying a large platter decorated with rose petals and lemon peel. In the middle is …

The Napolis are shouting. Mr. Angelou whistles. Samantha's jumping up and down and Anna beams. Nanna's laughing because she can actually hear the commotion.

"The middle. The middle." Samantha points excitedly.

There it is in all its glory. Jack's Ponto is perched on an overturned soup bowl. There's a tiny plate next to it with carefully sliced and fried Ponto shoots. "I can't believe this. It's crazy."

Mum's blond hair is fluffing into a cotton ball. She places the petaled platter onto the coffee table. "The famous Jack's Ponto appetizer," she announces. Everyone investigates, asks questions, until Mum says we can all take a sliver of Ponto, but NOT eat it yet.

"Before you taste Jack's Ponto, I want to say something in front of all of you." She coughs.

"Jack, whatever happens, I will always love you and think you're smart and brave and inventive." Her voice falters a bit. "You enrich my life ..." Mum looks around. "All our lives."

I can see Mr. Angelou smiling.

I love you too, Mum.

"All right. Let's see what the Ponto tastes like."

From the Author

My Jack books are inspired by my wonderful, crazy family and the people I love. When you read these books, I am inviting you inside my home to meet fantastic characters – Nanna, who is obsessed with buying bargains, the stepdad who is the best dishwasher in the whole world, the sister who loves dogs, the mum (me) who does the best jumping jacks possible, and of course, Jack.

I remember the time I was afraid to go to school because "the gang" surrounded me and stole my lunch. No one played with me. It was lonely and scary. I didn't feel I could ask my parents for help. They were both working so hard and tired ALL the time, so how could I bother them? As well as that, I was the older sister and I was supposed to be able to fix it up. I couldn't. And can you believe that it all happened to my son too? Did you know that one in six children are bullied in school? Well, I am a teacher, a specialist in Child Growth and Development, and an author. I was awarded the Order of Australia OAM and the best thing of all, I am a mother. Don't you dare tell my daughter or my son, but I just love my kids to death.

So I wrote *I Am Jack* for them and for all of you.

Visit Susanne Gervay's website at:
www.sgervay.com

Anti-Bullying Internet Resources for Kids:

www.stopbullying.gov/kids

www.PACERKidsAgainstBullying.org

Anti-Bullying Internet Resources for Parents:

www.stopbullying.gov/parents

www.pacer.org/bullying/

www.pta.org/bullying.asp

www.ala.org/offices/oif/foryoungpeople/
childrenparents/especiallychildren

www.adl.org/combatbullying

John Wood
founder of Room to Read endorses

Susanne Gervay's
I am Jack

www.roomtoread.org

Room to Read®

"*I Am Jack* is a wonderful book recognizing
the importance of kids, reading and literacy."

—Room to Read

There are more books about me and my family!